BEST

FRIENDS

IN LOVE

Rosie Rushton lives in Northampton. She took up writing because it gave her a wonderful excuse not to do the dusting and because the word processor was the only thing in the house that didn't answer back. Her three daughters managed to attain adulthood despite having the most embarrassing mother in Northamptonshire. She is passionately interested in family and relationship issues.

In addition to writing teenage fiction and running workshops in schools around the country, Rosie writes a weekly column for her local paper, contributes to a variety of national and local radio stations and writes travel features for national magazines, a somewhat remarkable feat for one who gets lost in a multi-storey carpark. Her two greatest ambitions are to write children's drama for television and see her first adult novel published before she is too old to look good in the publicity photographs.

Other books by Rosie Rushton, published by Piccadilly Press:

Best Friends – Together
Best Friends – Getting Sorted
Poppy
Olivia
Sophie
Melissa
Just Don't Make a Scene, Mum!
I Think I'll Just Curl Up and Die
How Could You Do This to Me, Mum?
Where Do We Go From Here?
Speak for Yourself
Staying Cool, Surviving School
You're My Best Friend, I Hate You!

FRIENDS

IN LOVE

ROSIE RUSHTON

PICCADILLY PRESS • LONDON

Text copyright © Rosie Rushton, 1999
Cover photographs © Ute Klaphake, 1998

Printed and bound by WBC, Bridgend
for the publisher by her in accordance with the
Copyright, Designs and Patents Act 1988.

Phototypeset from author's disc by Textype
for the publishers Piccadilly Press Ltd.,
5 Castle Road, London NW1 8PR

A catalogue record for this book is available
from the British Library

1 3 5 7 9 10 8 6 4 2

ISBNs: 1 85340 573 6 (trade paperback)
1 85340 597 3 (hardback)

Designed by Judith Robertson
Cover design by Mandy Sherliker

Chapter 1

LOVE LINES

"JASMIN, if you say '*love you to pieces, Sanjay*' just once more, I swear I shall scream!"

Chloë Sanderson poked her friend none too gently in the ribs and stabbed a purple varnished fingernail at her watch. "We're going to be late and . . ."

"Sssh!" Jasmin hissed back at her, clasping the telephone handset more tightly and turning her back on Chloë.

"Sorry, darling," she whispered down the line, "Chloë's being a pain."

She threw her friend a warning glance. Chloë gritted her teeth, sighed deeply and began tapping her foot impatiently.

". . . love you to pieces," murmured Jasmin. "Yes, really, really love you."

"*Really, really love you,*" mouthed Chloë, pulling a face. "For the last time, Jasmin, come on!"

Honestly, she thought, you'd think Sanjay and Jasmin had been apart for weeks instead of twenty-four hours. Jasmin's great but she doesn't have a clue: what does she know about emotional suffering? When I had to say goodbye to Jack . . . Stop it!

Chloë shook her thick mane of auburn hair impatiently as if the gesture would banish all thoughts of Jack Kempton from her mind. He was history. Bad news. A two-timing waster.

But she had loved him. So much. And now she had no one.

"No, you say goodbye first!" Jasmin was tittering down the phone. "No, you – go on, you hang up first."

"Oh, for pity's sake!" Chloë slammed her hand down on the telephone, cutting Jasmin off in her prime.

"CHLOË!" Jasmin wheeled round and glared at her. "How dare you! Now he'll think I hung up first."

"So?"

Chloë felt a pang of guilt at what she had done.

"So – we have this thing – you know, whoever hangs up last loves the most."

Chloë raised her eyebrows heavenwards. "How juvenile," she said in what she hoped were tones of mature sophistication. "Love is not quantifiable."

"Pardon?" Jasmin's furious expression turned to one of bewilderment.

"It's a quote – by someone famous," said Chloë knowledgeably. "And now, if you don't mind, can we go to the cinema? We are supposed to be having a girls' night out, if you remember."

Jasmin threw one last lingering look at the telephone and then grabbed her jacket and headed down the stairs which led from the Johnsons' flat to the busy café below.

"Except that it's going to be a girls' and boys' night out," corrected Jasmin as they dodged their way between the crowded tables towards the door. "Nick's coming."

Chloë looked at her in astonishment. "Nick? How come? It was supposed to be just us three – you, me and Sinead."

Jasmin shrugged. "Don't go blaming me," she said. "He came into the café earlier with his mum – did I tell you that Dad's made her manageress here now?"

Chloë nodded.

"Well, Nick said that Sinead had called him and asked him along tonight. He sounded dead chuffed."

"Oh . . . right." Chloë was surprised at how put out she felt at Sinead's boldness. "I can't think why – it's not a guy's sort of film."

Jasmin pushed open the door of the café. "What's got into you?" she demanded. "You're dead grumpy this evening."

"Sorry." It was easier to apologise – no way could she tell Jasmin, or anyone else for that matter, just why she was feeling so edgy these days, why there were days when she wished she was someone else – anyone, rather than Chloë Sanderson, daughter of the famous Suzy off the TV.

"It's OK," said Jasmin cheerfully, squeezing her hand. "Time of the month?"

Chloë inclined her head and made a non-committal sound in her throat. It seemed to satisfy Jasmin.

"Anyway, maybe it's not the film Nick's going for," Jasmin giggled, giving Chloë a sideways glance.

Chloë suppressed a smile and tried not to look smug. It was true that Nick had been keen on her for ages – ever since he started at Lockbridge High, in fact. Not that back then Chloë had taken much notice; she had been so wrapped up in Jack, so sure that theirs was a love that would last for ever. But now that Jack was gone – and good riddance, after the way he cheated on her – she had been thinking that it might be kind of nice to get it together with Nick. Nothing heavy, just someone to hang out with. He was, after all, quite a dish. And good fun. And she reckoned, with a bit of encouragement, he could be pretty romantic.

The more she thought about it, the more she liked the idea. "What do you mean – not the film?" she asked Jasmin, trying to look innocent.

"Well," said Jasmin confidingly, as they turned out of Water Street and quickened their pace towards the bus stop. "If you ask me, Nick's got a thing about Sinead."

"SINEAD?" Chloë blurted out, puckering her forehead. "I hardly think so."

"Why not?" replied Jasmin. "She's really nice and . . ."

"I know she is," agreed Chloë, "and I know she really

fancies Nick but, to be honest, well, actually he's always been more interested in . . ."

"What?"

Chloë couldn't say what she meant, even though she knew it to be true. "Football," she ended lamely.

Jasmin laughed. "And who organised the cheerleading team for the five-a-side competition? Sinead. And who sprung the surprise party to console them when they got beaten in the finals? Sinead. OK, so she's made a deliberate play for him – but I guess it's paying off."

Chloë chewed her lip and said nothing. If Jasmin was right, she was going to be the only one in their gang – probably in the entire Year Eleven – who didn't have a guy and that wasn't right. She'd always had a boyfriend, ever since Year Five of primary school; OK, so half of them had been spotty drips, nothing like Jack, but still.

She sighed. It was pointless thinking about Jack. He was probably right now conning someone else into believing his stupid lies.

Nick wouldn't lie. Well, not any more, and certainly not about things that really mattered. Nick was a really up-front kind of guy. And he did adore her. She knew he did.

"Here's the bus!" Jasmin nudged Chloë out of her reverie and sighed deeply. "It's going to be awful, you know."

Chloë frowned. "The film? It's supposed to be ace – it's had rave reviews."

"Not the film," said Jasmin, clattering up to the top deck, "being there on my own. Alone."

"You won't be alone, stupid," reasoned Chloë kindly, knowing how terrified Jasmin was of being anywhere dark on her own. "We'll all be there."

"But Sanjay won't," stressed Jasmin. "I miss him dreadfully. Being in love is so terribly painful, isn't it?"

Not half as painful as not being, thought Chloë ruefully as the bus pulled out into the evening traffic. But with a bit of luck, that situation wouldn't last much longer. Because she had made up her mind.

She'd get it together with Nick. Starting tonight.

Sinead had done her a real favour, persuading him to come along. And it was only fair that Chloë should make the situation perfectly plain. It wouldn't be fair to let Sinead think she had a chance with Nick. Much kinder to let her see how things stood right away.

After all, that's what friends were for.

Chapter 2

SCHEMES AND SURPRISES

NICK BOWEN was worried. Dead worried. In fact, he was beginning to wish he had never let Sinead persuade him into going to the cinema in the first place. There was no way he could go out of the house – not now. And worse still, he had a horrible feeling that if he wasn't on the corner at seven o'clock as he had promised, Sinead would come to find him. And that would be even worse.

He moved across his darkened bedroom and gingerly pulled back the curtain to peer out into the street. The man was still there, motionless on the other side of the road, staring up at the house. Nick couldn't make out his features in the darkness but he was tall, thick-set and, most worryingly of all, he was holding a sheaf of papers in his hand. Nick knew all too well what that meant. Someone else coming for money. Money they hadn't got.

He let the curtain fall back, and sank down on his bed. Clasping his hands behind his head, he stared up at the ceiling. Over the last few weeks he had actually begun to think that finally the whole wretched nightmare was coming to an end. Jasmin's dad had decided to make his mum manageress of The Canal Café, which meant a lot more money. They were even talking about moving out of his gran's house to somewhere of their own. And since the five-a-side football competition, he had felt that he finally belonged at Lockbridge High. But now this.

Nick had just got to his feet to check the window again when the doorbell shrilled. He jumped, and yanked back the corner of the curtain. The man had moved. He was no longer on the opposite pavement. He was standing under Nick's window and he had his finger very firmly on the bell.

Nick froze. He wouldn't answer the door. Then the stranger would have to give up and go away. For once he was actually pleased that his mum was working late; it meant that there was no car parked outside, no clue that there was anyone at home. His grandmother was away visiting her friend in Liverpool for the night; if she had been in the house there would have been no hope. Gran would entertain a runaway convict if it meant the excuse for a chat.

His thoughts were interrupted by the chiming of the grandfather clock in the hall below. Seven o'clock. Or more likely five past, since that clock was always slow. Right now he should be at the end of the road meeting Sinead. Be there or be oblong, she had said to him.

Despite his worries, Nick grinned to himself. She was like that, always saying dotty things that made him laugh. He'd never really taken that much notice of her, until she broke her ankle and couldn't be in the mixed footie team. Most girls would have whinged and whined, but she hobbled along to every practice, organising a wicked cheerleading team called The Lockets and brandishing her crutch in the air whenever one of Year Seven got out of step. Of course, she wasn't stunning like Chloë but she was a real laugh. Not that she would be laughing right now, he thought. Right now, she was probably heading down the street to give him what for.

The thought jolted him out of his reverie. The ringing had stopped. Pulling back the edge of the curtain, Nick sighed with relief. The man was crossing the street, stuffing the sheaf of papers into his raincoat pocket and casting a last reluctant glance at the house. He had clearly given up.

But he would be back. They always came back. After his dad had died so suddenly, it had seemed as if everyone they had ever known had beaten a path to their door, demanding that bills be settled and loans repaid. Bills and loans his mum had known nothing about. It wasn't that his dad was irresponsible, whatever his grandmother might think. It was just that he had bought three cottages in Tuscany and then died before he could turn them into holiday homes and make the mint of money he had always assured Nick was about to be theirs.

Which was why they had been forced to sell their farmhouse, why he had left his boarding school in Sussex and why they were now sharing his grandmother's cramped little house in Leeds. And why, if Nick was right in his suspicions, any dreams of their own house would be put on hold yet again.

He wouldn't tell his mum about the unknown caller. Just lately, she had begun to look really happy again and he didn't want that haunted look to come back into her eyes. After all, the man might not bother to come again. He might drop dead tomorrow. Anything might happen.

Nick cast a final glance up the street at the man's retreating back. And gasped. Hurtling down the pavement towards him, bag bouncing on her hip and hair flying, was Sinead. Any minute now, she would cross the road and ring his bell.

And if the man turned round and saw Nick answering the door . . .

Nick grabbed his wallet, flung open the bedroom door and leaped down the stairs, two at a time.

———

Sinead Flaherty slowed down to catch her breath and glanced at her watch. Eight minutes past seven. If her plan was going to work, they were going to have to move fast. Why hadn't he been on the corner? What had gone wrong? Please don't let him have changed his mind . . .

Calm down, she instructed herself firmly. You've got to play this dead cool. This, remember, is your masterplan.

She peered at the house numbers. Twenty-two, twenty-four . . . so Nick's must be on the opposite side of the road. She knew he lived at number thirty-three, not that she had ever been there before. In fact, none of their gang except Sanjay had been to his house; Nick wasn't the type to invite people home. Not even Chloë.

Sinead sighed. She knew just what she was up against; everyone knew that Nick was crazy about Chloë Sanderson. Not that she could blame him; she was the sort of girl who had it all; stunning looks, a model figure and loads of style. And she was nice with it. Not that Sinead had always thought so; they used to be deadly enemies until Chloë actually got her out of a couple of tight corners and stopped her from making a total idiot of herself. Which was why she would have felt guilty about her plan, if it hadn't been for the fact that Chloë had told her over and over again that she simply wasn't interested in Nick.

So, in a way, she was being fair all round; diverting Nick's unwanted attention away from her friend and offering Nick the unquestioning love he so clearly craved. She knew it was right; her stars had said so. *You have been harbouring a secret desire for weeks*, Deirdre Destiny had told her, *and with Mercury having changed direction, you can expect romance to look a whole lot rosier. But it's up to you to pursue your dream and give it all you've got!*

And that, thought Sinead, dodging a thick-set guy in a

raincoat and crossing the narrow roadway, is precisely what I'm going to do. Starting tonight.

Number thirty-three. This was it. She reached out her hand to the doorbell just as the door swung open.

"Sinead! You're here! Thank goodness!"

He certainly seemed pleased to see her, thought Sinead.

"Let's go!"

Nick grabbed her arm and manoeuvred her on to the pavement. He glanced quickly up the street and then pulled the door closed, clicking it quietly behind them.

"Quick!" He grabbed her hand and set off down the street at a such a cracking pace that Sinead had to break into a run to keep up with him.

"Hang on!" she gasped, but he merely tightened his hold and carried on. Not that she cared. He was holding her hand. And if they carried on at this speed they would be at the cinema well before Jasmin and Chloë got there. The plan was working.

They sped round a corner and Nick slackened his pace and let go of her hand.

"Sorry about not being at the corner," he said, with a smile that caused Sinead's stomach to embark on a series of somersaults. "I'm a terrible time-keeper."

"That's OK," she said, desperately trying to catch her breath. "I'm just glad you're coming."

Sugar. She shouldn't have said that. That was not cool or sophisticated or any of the other things that *Get Your*

Guy and Keep Him instructed you to be.

"It's supposed to be a brilliant film," she added hastily.

"It's not the film I'm interested in," he said, looking straight into her eyes.

Sinead's heart missed a couple of beats.

"Right now, the only thing that concerns me is getting as far away from Talbot Street for the evening as I can. Let's go."

Sinead sighed. So much for a declaration of love. Not that she had expected it. She had a lot of work to do on Nick before she could expect that.

But she had to start somewhere.

And there was no time like the present.

Chapter 3

THE BEST LAID PLANS . . .

"I CAN'T think where Sinead has got to," complained Jasmin for the fifth time in ten minutes. "I said specifically to meet us here by the sweet kiosk."

She peered round the crowded cinema foyer.

"Well, here or not, we'll have to go in," insisted Chloë.

"We can't," protested Jasmin. "We need to get four tickets together, otherwise we'll get split up."

"But the film's about to start. And they say the opening is mega-amazing – computer graphics gone wild!"

Jasmin sighed. "Just Sanjay's sort of thing," she murmured. "He's crazy about all that stuff. It feels all wrong not being with him on a Saturday. I shan't enjoy it half so much."

"So why didn't you ask him?" suggested Chloë, who had spent the entire bus journey listening to a catalogue of Sanjay's attributes, along with a complete rundown of the complications of a mixed-race relationship when you had parents as stuffy as Jasmin's. "Sinead clearly didn't care that it was meant to be a girls'-only night, so you could have done."

Jasmin raised her eyebrows. "His parents made him stay at home for some boring old dinner party," she said. "Flatly refused to reconsider. Weird or what?"

Chloë nodded. "My parents are only too pleased to get rid of me when they have friends round," she commented. "Mind you, the feeling's mutual."

Particularly as it's the only time I dare go out without worrying, she added silently to herself. At least if they've got visitors, I know nothing awful's going to happen. Which is more than I can for the rest of the time. Especially these days.

Stop it. Stop thinking about it. Just enjoy tonight.

She glanced towards the door. Still no sign of Sinead, and more importantly no sign of Nick either. Perhaps he was here already. Maybe he'd gone into the cinema, expecting to find her there, wanting a few quiet moments in the dark on their own. That would be it.

"Come on," she ordered Jasmin. "Enough is enough. We're getting our tickets and going in."

"But . . ."

"IN!" Chloë seized her friend by the arm and shoved her in the direction of the pay desk. "Two tickets for *If It Wasn't For You*, please."

The cashier looked up. "You're not Cleo and Janice by any chance?" she asked vaguely.

"Chloë and Jasmin," said Jasmin. "Why?"

"Your mates have gone in already – pretty girl, tall guy, yeah?" enquired the girl.

Jasmin nodded.

"Row H, seats thirteen and fourteen – she said to save them for you."

She waved two tickets at them. "Six pounds forty," she yawned, hooking a piece of chewing gum over her front teeth.

———

Chloë was halfway up the aisle in the cinema by the time Jasmin caught up with her. She scanned the rows and saw her friends almost at once.

And her heart sank.

Nick was sitting at the very end, in the seat next to the wall, and Sinead was next to him. She had a new hairstyle, a sleek bob with a touch of russet streaked through it and she was wearing a dead classy cropped jacket with champagne suede trousers. Chloë had never seen her look so good.

As she watched, Sinead leaned towards Nick and whispered in his ear. Suddenly Nick burst out laughing, throwing his head back and running his fingers through his thick, wavy hair. He looked so sexy. And now there was no chance of sitting next to him.

"You're crazy!" she heard Nick tease Sinead in what seemed to Chloë to be an unnecessarily affectionate manner.

"Hi there, you guys!" Jasmin pushed past her and shuffled along the row, flopping down on the seat next to Sinead. "You were meant to meet us in the foyer, remember?"

"Were we? Really?" Sinead turned a wide-eyed stare on Jasmin. "Gosh, I'm sorry – I didn't realise."

She smiled sweetly at Chloë, who had plonked herself reluctantly on the only remaining seat. "Hi, Clo – how's things?"

Catastrophic, thought Chloë, sinking further into the seat. Disastrous. Totally and absolutely the pits.

"Fine," she said. "Great." She tossed her head and ran her tongue lightly over her teeth, widening her eyes because everyone knew that was the height of allure. She leaned past Jasmin and Sinead. "Hi, Nick!"

But the lights were dimming and Nick only had eyes for the wide screen.

Just do it, Sanjay Fraser ordered himself sternly. Now. Just say it like it is and get it over and done with. Don't be such a total wimp.

"I'm not doing it, Dad, and that's that."

The moment the words were out he felt sick. His father stared at him in disbelief across the dining-table. His sister Rani, always sensitive to atmosphere, twisted the corner of her table napkin and chewed her lip. Only his mother, elegant in her emerald and gold sari, gave him a half smile and the very smallest wink.

"Well blow me, Duncan, the boy's got spirit!"

The cutlery rattled as their guest, Professor Felix Hadland, the dean of the university where his father was Senior Lecturer in American Literature, thumped the table with his fist.

"Sanjay!" His father's eyebrows met as he glowered across the table. "The professor has just offered to arrange work experience for you for with his brother, who just happens to be one of the country's leading barristers, and you have the audacity to . . ."

Sanjay clasped his hands tightly under the table to stop them shaking and turned to Felix. "I'm very grateful, sir," he began, remembering how Jasmin had told him that a bit of mild grovelling never went amiss. "But it would be wrong of me to waste your brother's time. I don't want to be a lawyer."

He took a deep breath, glanced at his mother who was paying great attention to her glass of wine, and went for the kill. "I did explain to Dad some time ago, but I don't think he believed me."

The professor did not look in the slightest bit fazed but merely inclined his head and nodded thoughtfully. Sadly, Sanjay's father was not so calm. "This isn't Sanjay speaking, Felix," he declared. "He's had a whole bunch of foolish ideas planted in his head by some trumped-up art teacher . . ."

"Information Technology, actually," interjected Sanjay's mother quietly.

"Whatever!" snapped his father. "The boy seems to think that he's actually going to earn a decent living drawing cartoons or some such rubbish and . . ."

Sanjay had had enough. He realised now why his father had been so adamant that he should be here tonight – so that he could try yet again to get him to do something he had no interest in. Well it wasn't going to work.

"It's not like that!" he shouted, and then deliberately lowered his voice. What was it Jasmin had said? Stay cool when they get aerated; it shakes them rigid.

"I want a career in animation," he said, turning to their guest and trying to stop his voice from wobbling. "You know, 3D stuff, teaching aids for kids with learning difficulties like Rani, that sort of thing."

"Fascinating," said Felix without a trace of sarcasm. "So tell me, what exactly are we talking about? Film making? Digital special effects? Computer animation?"

Sanjay opened his mouth to reply but his father got in first. "We're not talking about any of it, at least not here, and certainly not now," he said decisively.

"Pity," murmured Felix.

"Pardon?" queried Sanjay's father.

"Oh, I was just thinking that it's rather worrying when we academic types get so stuck in our ways that we can't be forward-thinking and open to technological developments."

Felix paused and broke a piece off his bread roll. "And even more worrying," he added mildly, "when talent is thwarted because of parental narrow-mindedness. Now, Dipti, my dear, is that some of your delicious lemon tart I see on the sideboard?"

———

Sinead clasped her hands to her mouth and gazed breathlessly at the screen. It was so romantic. One girl, fighting against all the odds, to reach the man she knew she was destined to love for eternity. A man who was hardly aware of her existence, who thought he was in love with someone else, someone who was quite clearly wrong for him. But for her love she was prepared to risk all. Right now she was in this jungle, being followed by two men who also wanted to reach this guy because . . .

"No!" She gripped the arms of her chair, unaware that she had shouted out loud when the python dropped from the tree and wrapped itself round the heroine's neck.

"Hey!" Nick covered her hand with his and squeezed it. "It's OK – it's only a film, silly!"

"What? Oh – sorry." Sinead flushed bright red. What a dork he must think she was! "It was just that I . . ."

She stopped.

His hand was still lying comfortingly on top of hers. Any minute now he would take it away.

She swallowed and smiled as tremulously as she could. And slipped her fingers between his, before turning her attention back to the screen.

Only now she wasn't really noticing the action at all.

———

She had action enough of her own right here. And she was enjoying it quite a lot.

_____

Would that guy come back? Had he just gone off for a coffee before trying again? Nick's forehead puckered into a frown. What if he knew that his mum worked at The Canal Café and went to find her there? What if he was confronting her right now? If he dared to upset her . . .

He felt his fists clench at the thought. And realised that he was still holding Sinead's hand. Somehow their fingers had become interlocked. He didn't quite know what to do. He wriggled them a bit and turned to glance at her.

At the same moment she turned and smiled at him and gave his hand a gentle squeeze. Her face was flushed and she seemed a bit breathless. Honestly, girls got so caught up in films – you could tell that python was computer-generated, just like the flash flood that had Sinead perching on the edge of her seat.

"You OK?" he asked.

"Yes," Sinead breathed. "Fine. Are you?"

Nick nodded and decided not to bother retrieving his hand. There were bound to be more scary bits in the film and if it made her feel better to hang on to him, why not?

He quite liked it anyway. Which came as something of a surprise.

_____

I'll kill her, thought Chloë. What does she think she's playing at? Nick might be taken in by her silly affected little scream but no one else was. Honestly, she's so blatant – doesn't she have any dignity?

She stuffed a handful of popcorn into her mouth and rammed the packet under Jasmin's nose. This wasn't how she had planned it. It should be her sitting next to Nick, legs crossed, mini-skirt hitched to just the right level above her knee. She would occasionally flick her hair over her shoulder and then fold her hands demurely in her lap, just out of reach. Tantalising, that's what you had to be. Not blatant, like Madam Flaherty.

Of course, Nick was probably as fed up with the situation as she was. Sinead had quite obviously cornered him, literally, and there wasn't much the poor guy could do about it.

"Told you!" Jasmin whispered, nudging her arm and jerking her head towards Sinead and Nick. "Love is in the air!"

"Which just shows how little you know!" retorted Chloë. "She's not his type."

Jasmin raised her eyebrows and gave a wry grin. "Oh, and you are, is that what you're saying?"

Chloë swallowed. "I didn't say that," she began.

"Well, to be fair, you did have your chance," Jasmin pointed out. "There was a time when Nick was drooling all over you and you hardly noticed him."

"SSSSSSHH!" an irate woman in the row behind

hissed in Chloë's ear. "Some people are trying to watch the film."

"Sorry."

Jasmin turned her attention back to the screen.

To Chloë's horror she felt her eyes fill with tears. Jasmin was right – she could have gone out with Nick any time over the last term and a half but she hadn't wanted to. She'd had Jack. And that had been enough.

But Jack was gone and now she wanted Nick. More than she would ever have dreamed possible.

Jasmin made it sound as if she had missed her moment. But that wasn't true, she knew it wasn't. She could still have Nick.

And she was going to have him. She deserved to have something go right in her life. Her mock GCSEs had been a total disaster, her teachers kept muttering about having a brain and not using it and at home you could cut the tension with a knife.

Besides, she hated the way she was feeling right now. Knotted up, and irritable, and at odds with the entire world.

What she needed was to be in love.

And she was going to make it happen if it was the last thing she ever did.

———

I shouldn't have said that, thought Jasmin. That was so mean of me. Something's wrong with Chloë and it's not just about missing Jack or being annoyed with Sinead.

She's been odd for days; really distracted and jumpy. And I've made it worse by drawing attention to Sinead and Nick. I guess Chloë's keen on him after all and now she feels jealous and left out. After all, not everyone is as lucky as I am. Not everyone can have someone as amazing as Sanjay.

She sighed. She liked to think of herself as Juliet, passionately in love with a guy her parents disapproved of, just because he wasn't African-Caribbean. They were so blinkered; Sanjay was living proof that mixed marriages worked. His mum was Hindu, his dad Canadian – and they were well balanced with it. They didn't throw a wobbly every time he went out with her. At least they weren't constantly thrusting other girls under his nose, not like her mum who insisted on introducing her to the sons of her friends and then singing their praises for days afterwards.

If Sanjay looked at another girl, I think I would die, she thought, stretching over and grabbing a handful of popcorn. I haven't seen him for twenty-six hours and thirty-five – no, forty minutes and it feels like an entire lifetime. I love him so much. I wonder what he's doing right now; I wonder if he's thinking of me.

I wonder if I could slip out to the loo and phone him. I could.

"Sorry," she murmured to Chloë. "Need the loo."

"But it's just getting to the really romantic bit," protested Chloë.

"I'll be ever so quick," Jasmin assured her.

Besides, no film can ever be half as good as the real thing. Poor Chloë. It must be awful not to know the meaning of true love.

———

"Is he furious?" Sanjay looked up from his computer as his mum pushed open his bedroom door. From below, he could hear the sounds of the dishwasher being loaded and drawers being slammed rather forcefully.

Dipti Fraser pulled a face. "Furious? no. Niggled, yes. Put out, definitely. He doesn't take too kindly to being contradicted, especially by one of his superiors."

"Sorry, but . . ."

His mum smiled. "I know, I know – and you don't have to apologise," she said. "You're right to stick out for what you want. And I don't think you'll find Dad pushing Law down your throat again."

Sanjay's eyes widened. "That's ace – you mean, he's said . . ."

His mum held up her hand. "Hang on," she interjected. "He hasn't *said* anything. I just have a feeling. Anyway, let's just take it one step at a time, shall we? You know your father – hates to admit he might have been wrong."

"But . . ."

"But give him time. Don't raise the subject for a while. There's no rush, after all, is there? It's not as if you have to make a decision tomorrow."

She ruffled his hair, and Sanjay grinned up at her. "I guess," he said.

In the hall below the telephone shrilled.

"It'll be for you," said his mum.

"How do you know?"

"These days," she said, winking at him, "it always is."

———

"That was brilliant!" enthused Nick as they pushed their way out of the cinema. "Great idea of yours, Sinead!"

"So where now?" enquired Chloë brightly, looking directly at Nick. "Fat Harry's? Or that new place in The Headrow? It's only nine thirty."

"Nine thirty?" Nick gasped, glancing at his watch. "Mum gets home by nine."

"So?"

Chloë could not see the significance of Jenny Bowen's timetable on her social life.

"So I need to be there – I mean, I promised to help her sort some stuff," he said hurriedly. "See you all on Monday – bye!"

"But . . ." Chloë began to protest but it was too late. Nick was already sprinting down the road.

Oh terrific, thought Chloë.

"I can't go on anywhere either," added Sinead.

It wasn't you I was asking, thought Chloë irritably.

"My dad's picking me and Jasmin up – do you want a lift?"

"Why not?" sighed Chloë, her eyes following Nick's

rapidly receding figure as it disappeared down the street. After all, there wasn't anything else to do except go home.

"So what's the score, then?" Jasmin nudged Sinead as they walked towards Mr Flaherty's blue Mercedes which was pulling up at the kerb.

Sinead frowned. "What do you mean?"

"Oh come on," teased Jasmin. "I saw you clutching Nick's hand as if your very life depended on it. So – has he asked you out?"

Chloë held her breath and tried to concentrate on not stepping on any of the cracks in the pavement.

"No," said Sinead shortly. "He didn't – we aren't – I mean, it's not like that."

Chloë's heart lifted. Of course! She saw it all now. The only reason that Nick had been in such a rush to get away was because he couldn't stomach any more of Sinead's clinginess. He was probably scared that if he went on to a club with them she would spend the rest of the night hanging round his neck like a limpet.

She gave a little skip and pulled open the rear door of the Flahertys' car. Sinead had actually done her a favour by throwing herself at Nick and scaring him off like that. No way was he going to fall for her little ploys in the future. From now on, he would be giving Sinead a wide berth. Which left the way clear for her.

"Hi, girls!" Sinead's father slammed the Mercedes into gear and grinned at them. "Good evening?"

"Lovely," sighed Sinead.

"Cool," said Jasmin.

"Oh yes," said Chloë with a cheery smile. "Very satisfactory."

Chapter 4

FAMILY FORTUNES

"NICK LOVE, get the door, will you? I'm in the middle of unpacking." His gran's voice wafted down the landing.

If his brain hadn't been scrambled by two hours of History revision, he might have stopped to think, but as it was, Nick merely slammed the book shut in relief, charged downstairs and slid back the bolt on the wooden front door.

"At last! I was beginning to think no one lived here!"

Nick gasped and swallowed. Standing on the step, leaning casually against the doorframe, was the guy who had been hovering across the street the night before. He was tall and broad-shouldered, with the tanned, chiselled features of someone who spends more time in the open air than at an office desk and he was dressed in an elegantly casual style that reeked of money.

"G'day to you, is this the Bowen household?" His voice had a faint Australian drawl.

Nick's brain sprung into overdrive. So this man was looking for his mother. But she wasn't here – she was working. And his gran was upstairs and hard of hearing.

"Bowen?" He frowned. "This house is owned by a Mrs Joan Andrews."

Well, it wasn't a lie. Gran did own the house.

The visitor frowned and pulled a wad of papers from the inside pocket of his jacket. "This is thirty-three Talbot Street, isn't it?"

Nick nodded, glancing up the road as he did so, just in case his mother had got away from the café early. It sometimes happened on Sunday afternoons.

"Well, that's odd," said the guy. "Oh, by the way, I'm Mike Lovell."

He stretched out a hand but Nick pretended to spot something on the floor and bent out of his way.

"Well," said Mike, "I guess I was wrongly informed. You don't know any Bowens round here, do you?"

"We haven't been here long," said Nick evasively. "We don't know many of the neighbours."

"Oh well, I guess it was a long shot anyway." He stuffed his papers back into his jacket pocket. "Maybe I should just give up. Anyway, thanks for your help."

He grinned broadly at Nick, and now that the threat was beginning to recede, Nick found himself smiling back.

"Look," said Mike, clearly encouraged. "If you do happen to come across anyone called Bowen, give me a call on this number, will you?" He scribbled on a piece of paper. "I'd really appreciate it."

"OK," said Nick, who had no intention of doing any such thing.

"Cheers." The guy waved and strode off up the street.

Nick shut the door and leaned back against it. He'd done it! He'd got rid of him before he could start pestering his mum. And what's more, the guy had talked about giving up.

"Who was it, love?" his gran called from the bathroom.

"Oh, just some guy wanting directions to that new health club," he improvised, crossing his fingers firmly behind his back. "Nothing important."

He sat down at his desk and tossed the piece of paper to one side. He'd done it. He'd put him off the scent. And so what if he did feel a bit guilty? He'd only done it to protect his mum and besides, that Mike guy didn't look as if he needed the money, even if they'd had it to give to him.

Which they didn't. Because every penny his mum earned was going to getting their own place. And then he'd be able to have a decent bedroom and invite his mates round. There was no way he'd ask Sinead over here.

He frowned, taken by surprise at his own thoughts. Sinead? It was Chloë he had always pictured sitting on the beanbag in the corner of his room, smiling up at him and hanging on his every word. Chloë whose arms he dreamed would one day be wrapped round him. Chloë who in the dark of the night he imagined kissing. Not Sinead.

Mind you, Sinead was a real laugh and she had been great over the five-a-side tournament. She was dead easy to be with because she didn't come on strong like some girls. She wasn't the type to want a guy to be all passionate and adoring. Which was just as well because, while he was frightfully good at chat-up lines and long, smouldering kisses in his dreams, he had never actually tried them out in practice with any success at all.

Maybe that was why he had enjoyed it so much last night. Sinead was just – well, Sinead. A mate. You knew where you stood with her. You didn't feel on edge all the time, worrying about whether you were going to put your foot in it or say something really naff. You could just be normal.

There was no point in dreaming about Chloë, anyway. She'd always been really nice to him, but she had made it clear a thousand times that Nick was just one of the gang. Even now that Jack guy was out of the picture, she still kept herself to herself, almost as if she didn't want anyone to find out too much about her.

Nick yawned and reluctantly opened his History text-book once more. He was, he thought wryly, about as bad at History as he was with girls. At least no one was going to put his sex appeal to the test in two months' time.

Firmly, he resolved to put all thoughts of love out of his head and tried to get excited about the Peasants' Revolt.

He had a nasty feeling it wasn't going to work.

———

Chloë lay on her bed, wishing she hadn't eaten so much Yorkshire pudding for lunch and listening to the muffled clattering of her father's ancient typewriter from his study at the bottom of the stairs. It was an irritating sound and yet one that gave her great peace of mind. Because as long as her father was battling away at yet another TV script, she knew from the noise exactly where he was. And that was how she liked it.

Her mum had offered time and again to buy her father a state-of-the-art PC, but Edward refused to bow to technology.

"If I wanted a word processor, I would buy my own," he had retorted only the afternoon before when Suzy thrust a PC World catalogue under his nose. "You may be earning more than me, but I'm not exactly destitute yet."

And then he had loomed over her, his eyes darkening and fists clenching in the way that always made Chloë feel physically sick.

"Get it?" he had asked in a low, menacing voice.

"But . . ." Suzy had begun and Chloë had rushed over to her, waving her Shakespeare text and begging for immediate assistance with a character sketch of Goneril and Regan. The moment had passed. For the time being.

Chloë didn't know how much more she could take. For the hundredth time in the last few years, she wished she had a brother or sister, someone who knew what it was really like to feel as if you were living on the top of a volcano that could erupt at any moment. And would. She knew it would. She had been through this so many times before that she could almost smell the build-up of tension in the house, hear the unspoken threats in her father's long silences and feel the desperation of her mother's frequent attempts to jolly him along, to do everything, anything to keep him on an even keel.

It had never worked for very long in the past. Chloë knew it would not work for very long in the future.

Sighing, she rolled off the bed and ambled to her desk. A pile of revision stared her in the face, revision she knew she had to crack if she was going to get decent GCSE grades. It was already the first week in March, and the exams began in early May. The trouble was, she didn't care any more. She wanted to care, she wanted to get all the old feelings back – the determination to get good grades, to pass her A levels and go to university and then to travel the world as a foreign correspondent. But what was the point? She was hardly going to go swanning off and leave her mother to face the music on her own, was she? For as long as *he* was around, Chloë knew that she would have to be too. And the worst thing about it was that there were times when she began to hate her father for what he was. For what he did. And for what he stopped her from doing.

"Chloë!" She ran to the door at the sound of her mother's voice. "Telephone, darling, for you."

Nick! Perhaps it was Nick; he often phoned on a Sunday – in the past, she had assumed that it was because he was stuck yet again on his German homework, but now she realised that it had been his way of hearing her voice, of feeling close to her. The poor guy had spent the previous evening itching to talk to her but totally unable to escape the clutches of Sinead. Well this time she would make it clear (subtly, of course) that she was available. She could almost hear the joy in his voice already.

She jumped down the two bottom stairs and grabbed the handset her mother had left lying on the hall table.

"Nick?" she gasped, catching her breath.

"You wish!" A suppressed giggle bubbled through the phone. "It's me, Jasmin."

"Oh," said Chloë.

"Well don't sound so thrilled about it," teased Jasmin. "Look, can you come round?"

"When?"

"Now. Or preferably sooner. Please."

Chloë heard the sudden catch in her voice.

"I need your advice," pleaded Jasmin. "I think my mother has just taken leave of her senses."

———

"They're at it again!"

Sinead looked up from her essay on Auden and into the pale face of her thirteen-year-old sister Erin. "At what?" she asked, slipping the top back on her pen.

"Oh you know – Mum saying that Dad's never at home, Dad saying that it's hardly surprising considering he's never allowed to move without her dusting up his footprints, Mum saying that it was his idea to live in a posh flat . . . you know."

Sinead nodded and sighed. She knew only too well. It was impossible – when they had all lived on the grotty Burnthedge estate and had a clapped out Vauxhall Vectra and a week's holiday at Butlins in Skegness, her parents were always laughing and joking. But when her mum had inherited loads of money from some dead cousin and they'd moved to this huge apartment in the same swish block as Chloë and had holidays abroad and a brand new Mercedes, not a week went by without some major bust-up between her parents. And her mum seemed so unhappy. When she had started as a voluntary helper at Rani's special needs school, Sinead had thought being among kids again would cheer her up. But it was only six hours a week and it wasn't enough.

"They won't get divorced, will they?" Erin's voice wobbled and she looked pleadingly at her sister.

"'Course they won't, silly!" Sinead jumped up and gave her a quick hug. Her sister could be a total pain most of the time – if prissiness was an Olympic event,

Erin would win gold, she thought, but she didn't want her worrying about something that wasn't going to happen. People didn't split up just because one of them spent all her time dusting and polishing and removing invisible marks off of skirting boards, and the other had chosen to set up a business making painted furniture that very few people seemed to want to buy. At least, she very much hoped they didn't.

Erin seemed reassured and strolled over to Sinead's dressing table, calmly helping herself to a generous dollop of her hand cream.

"My friend saw you last night," she said, casting a sideways glance at Sinead. "In the cinema. With a boy."

She made it sound as if Sinead had been caught safe-breaking. "Rachel says you were holding hands," she finished. "Were you?"

"And what if we were?" Sinead tossed her head and thought yet again what an excellent nun her sister would make. She certainly wasn't going to demean those magical moments with Nick by discussing them with Erin of all people. Just thinking about him brought back the feel of his hand in hers, the way his eyes crinkled at the edges when he laughed, the smell of him as he leaned towards her.

"You've gone all pink and soppy-looking," interjected Erin, abandoning the hand lotion and sampling Sinead's lip gloss. "Did he kiss you?"

"Erin!" Sinead retorted. "It's none of your business. And no, as it happens, he didn't."

She thought it politic to make this quite clear before Erin decided to spill the beans to their mother, whose ideas on boy-girl relationships hovered somewhere in the middle of the Dark Ages. Not that she intended to update her sister when the kiss finally did take place – which it would. She was going to make sure of that.

Her thoughts were interrupted by the slamming of a door followed by thundering footsteps.

"Shaun Flaherty, have you taken leave of your senses? What's possessed you to think of such a thing and you the father of two innocent young girls?"

Sinead and Erin exchanged wide-eyed glances and moved as one to the door. Their mother was standing at the bottom of the stairs, hands on ample hips, glaring at their father.

"And what have the girls to do with all this? They'll love it, sure they will," replied Shaun.

"What will we love?" demanded Sinead, running down the stairs, her sister hard on her heels.

Her father turned and beamed at her. "Toffee Apple, my sweetheart," he declared. "I've bought Toffee Apple."

Sinead wrinkled her nose. "I can't stand the things," she said, puzzled. "The toffee gets stuck in your teeth and . . ."

"Sadly," said her mother, sniffing in disapproval, "your father is not referring to an item of confectionary. It's a horse."

"A HORSE?" Erin and Sinead gasped in unison. "But you can't ride."

Shaun burst out laughing. "I'm not going to ride it, sillies," he said. "It's a racehorse – and I haven't bought all of it. Just a half share. With my mate Declan O'Connor."

"Really?" Erin's face lit up. "A real horse? What colour is it? Does it go really fast?"

"The only thing that goes really fast round here," retorted her mother, "is money slipping through your father's fingers."

Shaun's face clouded but he took a deep breath and touched his wife's arm. "Look, love," he said. "What's the point of having money if you can't enjoy it? We'll have the greatest fun – days out at the races, up to Maltby in the mornings to watch it on the gallops . . ."

"People like us don't own racehorses," declared her mother. "What's happened to you? And where's this going to end? I think you're taking leave of your senses! I almost don't recognise you any more . . ."

"Oh for pity's sake!" Shaun turned and yanked open the front door.

"And where do you think you're going?" Kathleen demanded.

"Out," said Shaun.

"Out where?" asked Sinead's mother.

"Anywhere without vacuum cleaners, furniture polish and women with long faces!" he retorted.

And slammed the door.

Sinead and Erin eyed one another. Their mother was

already plugging the cleaner into the wall socket.

"Tea, Mum?" asked Sinead, knowing that a cup of her favourite Darjeeling usually put her mother to rights.

"No thanks," said Kathleen briskly. "I've just finished cleaning my surfaces and don't want you messing them up again. OK?"

Sinead sighed. "OK," she said. But she very much feared that it wasn't OK at all.

Chapter 5

PARENT PROBLEMS

Chloë ran down the steps of her apartment block and headed off along the canal path to The Canal Café. She wasn't at all sure that she should be doing this, but at least it was only a couple of blocks away and she wouldn't be gone long. Besides, Dad had actually been humming when she left and that was always a good sign that the work was going well. Maybe his black mood really was passing.

She couldn't help feeling sorry for him in some ways – while her mum's career had really hit the heights in the last year, her father's was plummeting. His last sitcom had flopped and no one had bought any of his scripts for months. These days, if her parents went to a TV gala or awards ceremony, the pictures in the newspaper were always captioned *TV celebrity Suzy Sanderson and her husband Edward*. Her dad wasn't used to just being Suzy's spouse; he remembered the days when the *TV*

Times had billed him as *the funniest scriptwriter of the decade* and *the man who makes the nation giggle*. Not that living with him had ever been remotely funny.

"Thanks for coming!" Jasmin was waiting at the café door and grabbed Chloë's arm. "Upstairs. Now."

Chloë allowed herself to be dragged through the few remaining Sunday diners. "Hi, Mrs Johnson! Hi, Jenny!"

She waved cheerily to Jasmin's mum, who was talking earnestly to Nick's mother, busily polishing glasses at the bar.

"Hello, dear," began Nick's mum. "I hear you . . ."

But what she had heard Chloë never discovered because Jasmin had pulled open the door leading to their flat and shoved Chloë up the stairs.

"What on earth's going on?" panted Chloë as they reached Jasmin's bedroom and flopped down on the bed.

"Well, it's my mother . . ." sighed Jasmin wearily, kicking off her shoes and curling her legs under her.

"Not the Sanjay thing again?" asked Chloë, hoping that Jasmin was not about to launch into yet another account of her mother's antipathy to mixed-race relationships.

"No, it's not that – it's worse!" said Jasmin, then hesitated, biting her thumbnail in agitation.

"Well?"

"Well, it's just . . . I saw my mother . . . with a man . . . and they looked so . . . secretive, so . . ."

Jasmin swallowed and took a deep breath. "Oh, Chloë,

I just don't know what to think. I think maybe my mum's having an affair!"

———

Sanjay picked up the telephone, punched in a couple of digits, sighed and slammed the receiver down. What was the point? If he phoned Jasmin and her mum answered, it would only cause trouble between the two of them. And even if he managed to speak to her, the chances of her being allowed out to meet him were zero or less.

For a while it had seemed as if things were getting better. At Christmas time the gang had spent a lot of time at the café and he began to think that the Johnsons were accepting him. But then they had done their mock GCSEs, Jasmin hadn't achieved the grades her parents thought she should and suddenly they were saying it was all because the two of them were spending too much time together, that Jasmin was far too young to be consorting with boys and that from now on she had to knuckle down and apply herself to her studies.

Sanjay tore the top off the telephone pad and scrunched his doodlings into a ball, hurling them into

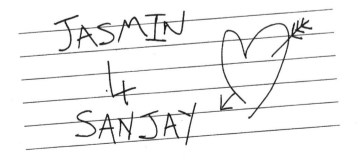

the wastepaper basket. At least it was only sixteen hours until he saw her again. He still found it hard to believe that a girl like Jasmin would actually say out loud that she loved him, that she wanted them to be together for ever, and that she was prepared to do anything to make sure it happened, parents or no parents. Not that they weren't both aware that they would have a struggle on their hands. Why did Jasmin's parents – and in particular, her stuffy mother – have to be so stressed out about the whole thing? He guessed that when you got to be over forty, you forgot what it was like to be madly, deeply, passionately in love and just got bogged down in convention.

It must be awful, he thought, as he dragged himself upstairs, to be that old.

———

"What should I do?" wailed Jasmin, looking at Chloë helplessly.

Chloë laid a hand on her arm. "Hang on," she said, trying to calm her friend down. "I mean, you're jumping to conclusions. OK, so tell me again – you saw your mum with this guy from the choir, right?"

"Yes. Mum's been away for three days singing in Scotland with the Gospel Choir. And when she came back it was in this guy's car. And, well, when she got out of the car he came round, picked up her hand and kissed it!" Jasmin wrinkled her nose in distaste. "And instead of slapping him round the face, like she should have done, my mother leans forward, hugs him and kisses him on the cheek. In broad daylight!"

Chloë frowned. "I'm sure it didn't mean anything," she said. "My mother hurtles around bestowing kisses on everyone, from the doorman at the TV studio to the cleaner's cat."

"She's a TV star, she's different," said Jasmin dismissively. "Besides, there's more – he gave her a red rose! A single red rose! And do you know what makes it even worse?" she exclaimed, starting to look angry now. "This guy is . . ."

Her words were lost in the din of an ear-splitting, teeth jarring crash. The two girls jumped out of their skin and were about to rush to the window when a cry went up from the quayside below. "Harry Johnson! What in the name of goodness . . . ?"

Whatever had caused the disturbance had clearly failed to amuse Jasmin's mother.

Jasmin threw open the window and leaned out, with Chloë peering over her shoulder.

Bobbing up and down on the canal below, and chugging intermittently, was a huge, rather ugly and very dilapidated narrowboat. And standing on the cabin roof, grinning from ear to ear and trying unsuccessfully to throw a rope over a mooring post was Jasmin's father.

"Ta-ra!" he called, waving his arms in a flourish and nearly toppling into the water. "So what do you think of her, then? Isn't she just amazing?"

Jasmin and Chloë looked at one another and without a word, turned and sped downstairs, through the café and out on to the waterfront. Jasmin's mother was standing, wide-eyed and speechless on the cobbles and a small crowd was gathering, watching with amusement as Harry inexpertly manoeuvred the huge barge up to the quay.

"There!" he cried proudly as he finally managed to secure the rope. He jumped ashore and gave his wife a bear hug. "How are you, my love?" he said. "Good trip? Choir in good voice?"

"I . . ." Words clearly failed even the usually vociferous Josephine.

"Dad," interrupted Jasmin, "what are you doing with a dirty old barge?"

Her father turned and grinned broadly. "That, sweetheart, is no ordinary barge. That is the *Josephine J*."

He bestowed a fond glance on his wife. "Named for you, my sunshine girl!"

Someone in the small crowd sighed romantically. Harry made a sweeping gesture with his arm. "This," he said, "is going to be our new cocktail lounge."

Jasmin eyed the peeling paint, the gaping hole in the cabin roof and the numerous dents in the bow before turning to Chloë and sighing deeply. "One parent going off the rails is bad enough," she muttered. "But two is more than anyone should be asked to cope with."

———

Surely Jasmin's mother isn't having an affair! thought Chloë as she ran up the stairs to her apartment. Mr Johnson's so sweet! And anyway, you couldn't really imagine someone of practically fifty being interested in – well, all that sort of thing. Love and passion and – well, sex – were for young people, people like her and Nick.

Nick and me, she thought, slotting her key into the lock and pushing open the front door. It's going to be so great – I can see it now; strolling along the canal hand in hand, his fingers gently flicking a strand of my hair away from my face before he leans towards me, cups my chin and . . .

"No, Edward, no! Please!"

Chloë froze.

From behind the closed kitchen door came the all-too-familiar sound of her mother's voice, trembling in fear and anticipation. The bile rose in Chloë's throat and for a moment her feet felt rooted to the floor.

"No, don't, Edward . . ."

And then life came back into Chloë's limbs and she sprinted across the sitting-room, throwing open the kitchen door and bursting through.

Her father was standing by the sink, his right hand clamped round her mother's slender wrist. He'd raised his left hand and seized a handful of Suzy's burnished brown hair, yanking back her head and pressing his face to hers.

"Stop it!" screamed Chloë. "Stop it now!"

Edward spun round, his eyes widening as his daughter advanced on him.

For a moment no one moved. Then Edward's hand fell to his side.

Chloë could feel her heart pounding in her ears, sense the damp sweat breaking out all over her body. She stared at her father, fury and contempt blazing in her eyes.

It was her father who looked away first.

———

Now that it was over, now that her father had gone, storming out of the flat in a rage, Chloë couldn't stop crying.

"I'm sorry, Mum," she sobbed. "I'm so sorry."

"Darling," soothed her mother, "it wasn't your fault."

"Yes it was," insisted Chloë. "He was in a foul mood yesterday; I should have guessed something like this would happen. I should never have gone out and left you."

Her mother smiled weakly and rubbed her bruised wrist. "No, darling, you mustn't think like that," she insisted. "Actually, it was my own stupid fault – I pushed him to it."

"MUM!" shouted Chloë, irritation taking over from her unhappiness. "You always say that – like there was any excuse for Dad to hit you, whatever you'd supposedly done."

Her mother sighed. "Yes, but you see, I told him . . ."

"I don't care what you told him," retorted Chloë.

"Mum, this can't go on. You have to do something. One day he's going to . . ." She stopped, unable to verbalise the terrible images that were darting through her mind. Large tears trickled down her cheeks.

Her mum leaned over, wincing slightly at the pain, and enveloped her in a hug. "It's all right, sweetheart," she said. "He doesn't mean it, you see. He loves me really. It's just that he's under a lot of stress right now."

She gave her another squeeze. "Now then, be an angel and pop the kettle on. Let's have a nice cup of tea and then we'll both feel better."

Chloë knew better than to argue. She dragged herself to her feet and did as she was told. But she knew full well that it would take more than a couple of cups of Earl Grey to take away the pain of what was happening.

Chapter 6

CHALLENGES AND CONFRONTATIONS

"A BOAT?" Sanjay looked incredulous. "Your dad has bought a boat?"

Jasmin nodded, grabbing a pile of books from her locker and thinking how unfair it was that the week should start with double Maths.

"What sort of boat? A dinghy? A cruiser?"

"Sadly not," sighed Jasmin. "It's a very ancient narrowboat with several large holes and a couple of broken portholes and my father imagines he's going to turn it into a floating bar. What's more, he thinks us lot can help paint the thing."

"Cool!" enthused Sanjay. "That is so . . ."

"Ah, Sanjay Fraser!" Mr Lamport, the headmaster, appeared from the staff-room door and clamped a hand on Sanjay's shoulder. "You and I need a chat."

"We do, sir?"

"Indeed we do – a long chat."

Sanjay swallowed and threw an anxious glance at Jasmin.

"Lunch hour in my study – no! No, sorry, can't do that. Make it after school – you can use the office phone to let your parents know you'll be late. Ah, Mrs Braithwaite, a word if you please . . ." And with that he strode off down the corridor.

"What was all that about?" asked Jasmin as they climbed the stairs to the classroom.

"Search me," shrugged Sanjay. "I can't think of anything I've done wrong."

Jasmin shook her head. "If it was that he'd have hauled you over the coals there and then," she said. "They like to get you first thing in the morning, so that they can make quite sure that they've ruined your entire day."

Sanjay grinned and then frowned. "I wish I knew what he wanted," he sighed.

Jasmin squeezed his arm. "Don't worry," she said. "It's probably something mega-boring like designing the cover for the school magazine or helping out at Junior Computer Club. One thing you can be sure of . . ."

"What?"

"It won't be anything remotely interesting. Old Lampost doesn't do interesting."

———

Sanjay's mother picked up the mail and padded through to the kitchen. She flicked through the assortment of envelopes and gasped.

She stood, frozen to the spot, fingering one of the letters and gazing at the postmark. "I can't open it," she told the goldfish, swimming calmly round and round in its bowl. "Supposing . . . ? But then again . . ."

Closing her eyes and taking a deep breath, she ripped open the envelope and pulled out the single sheet of paper. Biting her lip, she peeped at it through half-open eyes. And shrieked out loud.

"Yes! Yes! They've said yes!"

She clamped her hands to her mouth and did a little dance on the spot. "Oh, my goodness! Oh dear heavens! I did it! I DID it!"

Her eyes scanned the letter again. "Just wait till I tell Sanjay and Rani! They'll be delirious. And Duncan . . ."

She paused, a frown clouding her face. She put the letter on the table and slowly poured herself a cup of tea.

Telling Duncan would be interesting. Because one thing she knew above all else. Her husband would be far from delighted at her news.

In fact, he would probably burst a blood vessel at the very thought of what it might all lead to.

———

Until now, Chloë had always considered Monday mornings to be the pits. Double Maths followed by double History was hardly the stuff that dreams were made of – unless, like today, you happened to be sitting just two metres away from Nick Bowen, watching the way he ran his tongue along his bottom lip when he was concentrating, and wondering how it would feel to run your fingers through his wavy brown hair. And, as an added bonus, Sinead wasn't in their set for Maths or History which meant that Chloë had until lunch-time to come up with the perfect chat-up line, to let Nick see that she was available and that he no longer had to suppress his feelings for her, without Sinead jabbering on at him nineteen to the dozen. He hadn't been particularly chatty when they had bumped into one another after registration – but then, she guessed he needed some gentle coaxing, some reassurance that this time his advances would not be rejected.

She sighed. He was so fit – and it would be wonderful to have a boyfriend again, someone who would adore her and make a fuss of her, someone who would help her forget the mess at home, someone who would occupy her heart and her mind and give her something else to think about other than the fact that she just knew she was going to flunk her exams and when her father was going to flip again.

"Nick!" Mr Tompkins waved a ruler in the air. "Question eleven, page thirty-two – the answer, if you please."

Nick, who clearly had been occupied with thoughts that had little to do with Mathematics, looked flustered.

"Five point eight," hissed Chloë, leaning back in her chair and whispering out of the corner of her mouth.

"Five point eight, sir," said Nick.

"Well, well, you do surprise me!" exclaimed Mr Tompkins. "A right answer first time – things are looking up, Mr Bowen."

He turned to write on the board and Nick threw Chloë a grateful glance. She smiled back in what she hoped was a suitably smouldering manner, crossed her legs and winked at him. His face turned scarlet and he suddenly became deeply engrossed in his Maths folder.

No matter. He knew – and she knew he knew. From now on, it would be plain sailing. She had Nick Bowen in the palm of her hand. And it was a very exhilarating feeling.

———

While her daughter was savouring her newfound feelings, Suzy Sanderson was bringing 'The Breakfast Break' to a close. "And tomorrow," she said brightly, giving camera three her broadest smile, "I shall be talking to some of Britain's top sports stars about the forthcoming MegaSportUK festival . . ."

She turned to face camera two, wincing at the shaft of pain that gripped her bruised neck.

Keep the voice steady, she told herself. Breathe deeply. ". . . I'll be interviewing three men who plan to retrace the steps of Hannibal over the Alps – complete with elephants. You think I'm joking?"

She raised an eyebrow and gave her famous wink to camera. ". . . and we'll be finding out about the latest fashion news for summer. So until tomorrow at seven thirty, this is me, Suzy Sanderson, saying go easy on yourself and have a laugh!"

She held her smile until the light on the camera dimmed, the studio staff sighed with relief and Nathan, her producer, bounded across the floor towards her.

"Lovely, my dreamboat, lovely!" he enthused. "But then again, whenever are you anything but divine!"

"OK, Nathan," she sighed wearily, "you can cut the flattery. What do you want?"

Nathan ran a hand through his hair. "Well, my love, I was just wondering – I know you want to dash home . . ."

Oh really? thought Suzy. Right now, home is the last place I want to dash to.

". . . but could you just stay for an hour or so longer? I need a quick editorial meeting and without you it's a pointless exercise."

"Of course I'll stay, Nathan," said Suzy brightly. "Let me grab a coffee and I'm all yours."

Nathan's face creased into a smile. "You're a gem, Suzy," he said. "And I promise I won't take more than an hour. Then you can be off."

"Take as long as you need," said Suzy. "I'm in no rush to get back."

In fact, she thought wearily, I sometimes dream of never having to go back. Ever again.

She shook herself.

How ridiculous! How selfish! After all, Edward was

just going through a bad patch and besides, she had Chloë to think of and even if . . .

No. Don't think about the even ifs. Just keep on working. Things will get better.

She fingered the pile of papers in her shoulder bag. If this new project worked out, maybe she could . . .

"Suzy!"

She snapped her bag closed and looked up brightly. "Coming, Nathan! Right away!" she called.

———

That was just so typical of me, thought Nick as he pushed his way up to the tuck shop counter at break-time. OK, so I'm not that hot at Maths, but it was only because I was thinking about that Mike guy and wondering how much money he's after; that's why I couldn't think straight. And then not to be able to think of something really slick and witty to whisper back to Chloë – that was so dorkish! She must think I'm a right nerd.

"Are you going to spend all day gazing at these chocolate bars or could you force yourself to make a purchase?"

The woman behind the counter gave him an irritated glance.

"Sorry – I'll have a . . ."

"We'll have two Walnut Whips and a KitKat!"

He turned to find Sinead thrusting a pile of coins over the counter and grabbing her purchases. "Come on," she said cheerfully. "It's serious calorie consuming time!"

He grinned, shook his head and followed her out into the playground and across to the grassy bank that overlooked the tennis courts. "How did you know I like Walnut Whips?" he asked.

"Considering you consumed them like they were going out of fashion all the time we were at the five-a-side tournament, it was hardly rocket science!" Sinead grinned. "Here – indulge!"

She thrust one into his hands, peeled the paper off her own and stuck her tongue into the soft filling. "Bliss or what?" she sighed.

Nick burst out laughing.

"What?"

"How come you have one lick and get chocolate all over you?" he teased. He tapped the end of her nose with his finger.

Sinead looked at him, wide-eyed.

He swallowed. For some unknown reason his heart was beating rather faster than usual and he had a sort of pins and needles feeling in his chest.

He was just thinking that he had never noticed what lovely hair Sinead had – all sorts of different colours merging into one and little wispy bits catching the sun light – when suddenly she burst out laughing and rubbed her nose and wiped chocolate on to her school skirt.

"You're crazy!" he told her, giving her a friendly shove. "Dead daft and totally dotty."

"It comes with years of practice," grinned Sinead.

And Nick smiled back at her, warmly.

———

"Sure, he's a fine colt!" Shaun Flaherty stood, hands on hips, gazing at the sprightly two-year-old with pride.

"You're right there, it's a lot of prize money we'll be winning with that one," agreed his mate Declan, rubbing his chin in satisfaction. "Kathleen will be proud of you."

"Not really. Kathleen doesn't quite approve . . ." Shaun replied with a wry laugh as they walked over towards the stable offices.

It was odd. Now that they had everything they'd ever wanted – and more – they'd lost something vital in the change. Ever since they came into the money, Shaun had felt his wife slipping away from him. Not into the arms of another man, not into some new high-powered career – both of those he could have fought and had a chance of winning.

No. Kathleen was slipping away and he didn't know where she was going. All he knew was that she was changing. The kids had seen it, he could tell that from the way they eyed her warily every time she yelled at them to take their muddy shoes off or fold their magazines away.

Sinead had hinted once, a few months back, that her mum was depressed. But then she had taken that part-time job at the special school where the little Fraser girl went, and for a while she seemed happier.

But now . . . Don't be daft, Shaun told himself. Depression is what you get when things keep going wrong. People who lived at The Wharfside and had money coming out of their ears and no need to work ever again didn't get depressed.

It was the menopause, that's what it would be.

Vitamins. He'd get her some vitamins. That would put her right.

"So, that's four thousand, five hundred you owe me, please!"

The voice of John Spiers, the trainer, interrupted his thoughts.

"Four thousand, five hundred?" The words were out before Shaun could stop them. It did seem an awful lot of money, on top of the thirty thousand they had paid only last week for the horse.

"Your colours, and registration at Wetherbys, and the first month's training and feed, and the vet's inspection, and . . ." The trainer tapped his fingers as he listed each item.

"And there's me forgetting my cheque book!" gasped Declan, clamping a hand to his forehead. "Shaun, can you pay the lot and I'll settle up later?"

"Sure I can," smirked Shaun, eager to make up for sounding so tight-fisted. "Now, John, what about that little race at Doncaster in April? Perfect for our Toffee Apple, wouldn't you say?"

———

I'll kill her, thought Chloë, eyeing Nick and Sinead from the opposite side of the playground. Just who does she think she is? I'm going to go across there and . . .

"What's wrong?" Jasmin appeared at her elbow, sucking cola through a straw and munching on a cheese bap. "You look like you're about to commit murder."

She followed Chloë's gaze across the playground. "Ah," she said. "I get it. So what are you going to do about it?"

Chloë tossed her head and tried for the cool, sophisticated look. "Do?" she asked. "About what?"

"Very good," applauded Jasmin. "But you don't fool me for a second. You want Nick."

"You have such a subtle way of putting things," retorted Chloë, giving her a rueful smile. "Yes, I guess I do want him. And I'll get him."

"But Sinead's really . . ."

"Sinead," said Chloë graciously, "is great. I like her a lot. But she's not Nick's type. Believe me, I know about these things."

Jasmin did not look convinced.

"Don't worry," Chloë assured her. "I shall be charm personified. I shall let her down really gently. In fact, I'll . . ."

Her words were drowned by the sudden ringing of the electronic bell announcing the end of break. She glanced across the playground. Nick had stood up, and was holding Sinead's hands, pulling her to her feet. As he did so, Sinead toppled and brushed against Nick's arm. He leaned across and brushed grass cuttings from her skirt.

Chloë felt her fists clench. "God, she's so blatant, so tarty, so full of herself . . ."

She stumbled to find words strong enough to express her feelings. "I'll kill her!"

Jasmin raised her eyes. "If this is charm personified," she said with a grin, "I dread to think what you're like when you're being beastly!"

Chloë swung round – and realised that Jasmin was grinning at her. She gave a slightly embarrassed laugh. "OK, OK," she said. "Maybe I won't kill her."

She paused and slipped her hand through Jasmin's arm. "But I'm still going to get him," she said. "In the nicest possible way."

———

"Some enchanted evening, you will see a stranger, you will see a stranger, across a crowded room. And somehow you'll know . . ."

"You're sounding cheerful this morning, Josie!" Jenny Bowen dumped a pile of baguettes on the kitchen table and grinned at Jasmin's mother. "Mind you, not every woman has a boat named after them!"

Josie threw her a warning glance. "Don't you mention that heap of floating rubbish!" she warned. "Honestly, what possessed Harry to do such a thing? It'll take for ever to convert it. And where is the money coming from, you tell me that?"

Jenny shrugged, surprised at Josie's offhand manner. "Oh, I guess he's got that sorted," she said. "You must admit, it's going to be a real draw to the punters. I was thinking, we could serve a whole assortment of butties – you see, in the old days a butty was a boat that . . ."

"Jenny, serve what you like. You're the manageress. You're the one who seems able to get excited about this place. Only just don't drag me into it, OK?"

Jenny eyed her, opened her mouth and then clearly thought better of it. "Oh well, I must get going – we're starting those new basket lunches today."

She turned and looked at Josie. "And don't worry," she urged. "Harry's not the type to rush headlong into something without giving it a lot of thought, is he?" Without waiting for an answer, she pushed open the door and headed into the café.

No, thought Josie, half-heartedly chopping some yellow peppers, he's not. He's not one to act on impulse, to do something crazy just for the sake of it without thinking of the consequences. Neither am I – or rather, neither was I. Until now.

But dare I go through with it? It feels so right – but is it worth the risk? And how will I tell Harry . . . ?

"There you are!" Harry's booming voice caused Josephine to jump out of her skin. "Leave all that and come outside! I want to show you all over the boat."

"You make it sound like the *Sea Princess*," retorted Josie. "And besides, I've these salads to do and . . ."

"Oh, Anton can do those!" He threw open the café door. "Anton – here – now!"

He took Josie's hand. "No point employing an underchef and then chopping peppers yourself," he grinned. "Now, come on – we'll take a bottle of wine on to the deck and I can tell you what I plan to do."

He dragged her through the door. "And then you can tell me all about your choir weekend," he added hastily. "Yes?"

"Mmm," said Josie, thinking, But what do I say?

―――――

"Go on," urged Jasmin, pushing Sanjay towards the headmaster's door. "He won't eat you."

"I know," said Sanjay, "I just can't think what it can all be about."

"Well," reasoned Jasmin, "if you go in there, you'll find out, won't you? I'll wait for you. I know you've got your bike but I want to know that everything's OK."

"Thanks." Sanjay smiled gratefully and knocked on the door.

"Come in!"

"Good luck!" whispered Jasmin and settled down on the bench outside the headmaster's study to wait.

―――――

"Nick!" Chloë touched his arm as he headed for the school bus. "I wondered – are you doing anything tonight?"

"Me? Oh just Biology, French translation, that

impossible Geography essay, loads of revision . . . the usual!"

Chloë flicked her hair behind her ear and smiled sweetly. "Exactly," she said. "So what I was thinking was that you and I could work together – you know, pool our resources. We could get the essay done in half the time, and then test one another on the revision. What do you say?"

"You mean . . ."

"I could come over to your place and . . ."

"No!" Nick almost shouted the word. "I mean, it's not convenient, my mum – that is, my grandmother has visitors and . . ."

"OK," said Chloë easily. "You come to me." After all, she thought, it would be OK. Her father had gone on an overnight trip to Glasgow and her mum was forever going on at her to invite more friends home.

"Well . . ." Nick floundered. "Yeah. Yeah, OK. Cool. What time?"

Chloë thought fast. She needed time to wash her hair, do her nails, get her make-up on . . . "Say half past seven – after you've eaten. Is that all right?"

Nick nodded. "Sure," he said. "See you then. I hope you know more about rift valleys than I do."

If I have my way, thought Chloë, clambering on to the bus and smiling smugly at the sight of Sinead sitting on the back seat with her head in a magazine, rift valleys will be the last thing on your mind.

———

"But, sir, I can't – I mean, I never thought about . . ."

The headmaster clasped his hands behind his head and leaned back in his leather chair. "Well, now is the time to think very seriously about it, Sanjay," he boomed. "I haven't misread the situation, have I? This is what you want to do?"

"Oh yes, sir," Sanjay assured him. "But my father . . ."

"Ah yes, your father!" Mr Lamport rubbed his chin thoughtfully. "Mr Buckley told me there was a slight difference of opinion in that quarter."

He picked up a pencil and began tapping the top of his desk. "You know, Sanjay, there comes a time in all our lives when we have to go for it – stand up for what we believe, give it our best shot."

He leaned forward. "And now is the time for you, Sanjay. Tell your father what I have said. Discuss it with him. You want to do this, don't you?"

"Well, yes, sir – but I mean – can't it wait? I mean do I have to . . .?"

"Sanjay Fraser!" Mr Lamport stood up in exasperation. "Sitting on the fence never got anyone anywhere. This opportunity won't come again, believe me. It's only because an ex-university chum of mine brought it to my attention that you've got this chance at all. And time is running out."

He picked up the glossy brochure lying on his desk. "Now look at this – page seventeen, I think it was . . ."

———

Jasmin looked at her watch in agitation. Ten past four. Sanjay had been in with the head for thirty minutes. What could be going on? If he didn't come in five minutes, she would have to go. There was only one more school bus to The Wharfside.

Come on, Sanjay, come on. It can't be that earth-shattering, surely?

———

"Well, now," said Mr Lamport, "do you see why I was so excited for you?"

Sanjay nodded eagerly. "Oh yes," he breathed. "It's amazing. Simply amazing."

"So you'll talk to your father? Here, take the brochure – and remember, I must have an answer one way or the other by Friday at the very latest. Preferably before."

Sanjay swallowed, his stomach fluttering partly at the mind-blowing concept the headmaster had hurled at him, and partly at the thought of confronting his father. It was all pretty pointless really. He knew already what his reaction would be.

But his mum would be on his side. Maybe she could persuade him.

Mr Lamport was right.

He had to give it a go.

If he didn't he'd never forgive himself.

———

It was no good. She would have to go.

Jasmin stood up and gathered her books. The last bus,

held back for pupils in detention or doing Gym club, was already revving its engine.

She ran across the playground, casting the occasional glance over her shoulder to the swing doors.

There was no sign of Sanjay.

She jumped on to the bus and turned once more. As the doors closed behind her, she caught sight of Sanjay rushing through the double doors, waving wildly.

The bus edged forward on to the busy road.

"Sugar!" muttered Jasmin, sinking down into the last available seat. Now she would have to wait until she could phone Sanjay in order to find out what had been going on.

And that meant making sure her mother was out of earshot. No way was she going through another one of those "work matters more than boys" sessions that her mother was so keen on.

It was a pity, she thought, that her sainted mother couldn't practise what she preached. One thing was certain – if her mum gave her any more grief over Sanjay, Jasmin was going to tackle her about what exactly *she* was doing.

She had no right to stop her daughter following her heart.

———

Sanjay yanked his bicycle out of its stand and undid the padlock. He half wished that Jasmin was still around so that he could sound her out about this mind-blowing idea that Lampost had come up with. On the other hand, in some ways it was a relief that she wasn't. He couldn't bear to think how devastated she would be. He could almost hear her pleading with him not to do it, not to think about it.

Not, of course, that he would be doing it. For one thing, his father wouldn't hear of it. And for another, he wasn't the sort of guy that could cope with something as way out as that.

He jumped on to his bike and pedalled furiously out of the school gates and on to the main road. He tried to put the whole thing out of his mind, but a mass of thoughts kept crowding into his brain, possibilities that he had always thought were just stupid daydreams were taking shape inside his head, and his chest was almost bursting with excitement.

There wouldn't be any harm in giving it a go. Just taking a closer look, seeing what it would be like.

It wasn't as if he expected to go through with it.

And Jasmin wouldn't mind, just as long as she knew he wasn't serious.

He'd give her a ring later, he thought, turning into Marsh Lane. Sound her out.

But first, he had to confront his father.

The thought was so off-putting that he wobbled precariously and almost fell off his bike.

Chapter 7

WORRYING DEVELOPMENTS

"HI! I'M BACK!" Nick burst into the kitchen to find his grandmother and mum deep in conversation over a cup of tea.

"Such a lovely man, he was!" his gran was saying. "Charming manners, you know?"

"What man?" Nick's brain went on red alert. "Who?"

His mum looked up. "Did you have a good day, darling?" she said. "There's some tea left in the pot if you . . ."

"What man?" Nick repeated urgently. "What's gran on about?"

His mum looked surprised. "Just some guy who called, asking for me," she said. "I've been racking my brains to think who it could be – Mr Lovell, did you say?"

She turned to Nick's gran, who nodded.

"Mark, was it?" she murmured. "Martin?"

"Mike," said Nick without thinking.

His mother and grandmother looked up in surprise.

"You know him?" Jenny Bowen was frowning.

"I – er – well, no, it was . . ."

"So it *was* you!" His grandmother stood up, eyeing him with a degree of irritation. "He said he'd called before and spoken to a young lad who said there were no Bowens living here . . ."

"I DID NOT!" retorted Nick. "I simply said the house was owned by a Mrs Andrews. Which it is."

"Huh," snorted his grandmother. "Well, anyway, I put him straight. I said yes, my daughter and grandson were stopping with me . . ."

"You did what?" Nick gasped. "Gran, how could you be so dumb?"

"NICK!" His mother stood up. "Apologise to your grandmother this instant."

"Sorry." Nick looked at the floor.

"But, Nick, why?" asked his mother. "Why didn't you tell him the truth? This poor guy has apparently been wasting days trying to track me down and you tell him a bare-faced lie . . ."

"And to think I was blaming that little lad Barney who does my windows," sighed his grandmother.

"I wonder what he wanted?" mused Jenny, biting into a second slice of ginger cake and licking her lips appreciatively. "Mike Lovell – you know, I have a feeling that name rings a bell, but I can't place it . . ."

"For heaven's sake!" Nick lost his cool. "Can't you see? It's sure to be someone else coming for money that Dad owed them. That's all the so-called visitors we ever get these days, remember?"

His mum's face reddened and immediately Nick felt terrible. "I was trying to – oh, I don't know – buy some time or something," he said miserably. "I thought that he might lose interest and give up. I only did it to protect you."

Jenny smiled weakly and then looked serious. "Nick, if he has come because we owe him money, we will work out a way of paying it," she said. "We are not going to hide away in corners or start telling lies to get ourselves out of trouble."

"Trouble caused by that no-good Greg . . ."

"MOTHER!" Jenny's voice stilled her mother instantly.

She took a deep breath. "Did he say when he would be calling back?"

Nick's grandmother shook her head. "I was about to ask him in . . ."

Nick raised his eyebrows.

". . . when one of those awful mobile phone things rang and he said he had to dash to some meeting or other. Called me ma'am, he did. Lovely manners."

"Let's hope you feel the same when he demands a whole load of cash," retorted Nick.

"Maybe it's not about that at all," suggested his

mother, but she didn't sound very convinced.

"Maybe," said Nick, "a pair of pink pigs will fly past the window any moment now. I'm going upstairs."

His mum stared after him, trying hard to ignore the slightly sick feeling in her stomach. Mike Lovell. Mike Lovell. She had heard that name before. It must be someone Greg had known in Italy. Which meant that Nick was probably right.

She could feel her mouth going dry, the familiar tightening of her chest. Please no. Not again. Not when she was so close to saving up a deposit for a place of their own.

It wasn't fair. It wasn't me who had squandered all that money, she thought. But it's me who is having to pick up the pieces, me who is having to start from scratch again. Not you, Greg. Not you. No worries for you where you've gone, are there?

Angry tears filled her eyes, and she brushed them away before her mother could see them. She shouldn't be angry with her dead husband. She had loved him. Did love him.

But she didn't like what he had done. Not one little bit.

———

"Chloë, hang on!" Jasmin jumped off the bus and grabbed Chloë's arm. "Look, I need to ask you a favour."

"What?"

"Come back to the café with me and do your charming bit with my mother. Please."

Chloë looked at her in astonishment. "Jasmin, what are you on about?"

Jasmin took her arm. "I need to phone Sanjay," she said. "My mother will go ballistic, right? She's got this new rule – no phone calls till homework is done. Dead archaic."

"Sounds it," agreed Chloë, quickening her pace along The Wharfside.

"But if you're there, and I say I'm dashing upstairs to get you a book to borrow or something, and you stay and talk to her . . ."

"You can phone the beloved Sanjay and she'll be none the wiser," concluded Chloë.

"So you'll do it?"

"No."

Jasmin's eyes widened. "What do you mean, no? It's hardly international espionage."

Chloë grinned. "I would but I've got to dash – Nick's coming round later," she said proudly, as they reached The Canal Café.

"So?"

"So I have to get ready and . . ."

"Chloë," said Jasmin. "Who was it who sent e-mails halfway round Europe for you? Who was it who got into trouble with her parents when . . ."

"OK, OK, point taken." Chloë looked abashed. "But you'll have to be quick about it – none of these hour-long phone calls and kisses down the line."

Jasmin grinned. "Promise," she said, pushing open the door. "Look, there's Mum over in the corner and . . . oh no! I don't believe it!" She stood stock still in the doorway, gawping across the room.

"What?" Chloë edged past her.

"Him. There. With her."

Jasmin jerked her head towards the far corner of the café. "That's him," she breathed, swallowing hard and gripping Chloë's wrist. "The man she was with before."

Chloë peered across the room. Sitting opposite Mrs Johnson, wearing an impeccably tailored silver-grey suit, was a slim man with greying hair. Jasmin's mum was leaning towards him, quite clearly hanging on his every word.

"But," began Chloë, "your mum wouldn't be having an affair with him. I mean, he's . . ."

She stopped, horrified at what she had been about to say.

"Exactly," said Jasmin, eyeing her closely. "He's white. Now do you see what I mean about my mother being a total hypocrite?"

Chloë swallowed and said nothing. It seemed best that way.

"Well, go on!" Jasmin shoved her in the back. "Go – and find out all you can, OK? I'll be two minutes."

"But, Jasmin, you can't just go and leave me . . ." Chloë protested.

But she had.

———

"So what happened?" Jasmin lowered her voice and gripped the receiver.

"It was amazing," began Sanjay. "Apparently, there's this college, down in London, with this amazing course where . . . hang on."

Jasmin waited.

"Look, I can't talk now – if Dad gets to hear what Mr Lamport said, he'll go ballistic."

"Why? You're not in trouble, are you?"

"No way," replied Sanjay. "Look, can you come over?"

"Well, I . . ." Jasmin glanced out of the window at the dark street below.

"Oh no. Sorry. Forgot."

There was a pause and Jasmin could imagine Sanjay tapping his fingers in irritation. Why was she such an idiot?

"I could come to you but I guess it's . . ."

"Not a good idea," agreed Jasmin. "But look, how about we meet somewhere?"

"But – the dark . . ." began Sanjay.

"You're more important," announced Jasmin bravely, racking her brains to think of somewhere nearby. "How about we meet outside Chloë's apartment block in twenty minutes? You know where I mean?"

"The Wharfside? Great," said Sanjay. "If you're sure."

"Positive," said Jasmin.

OK, so she cheated, she thought, as she replaced the receiver. She could walk home with Chloë and she knew

Sanjay would walk her back.

But it was a start. She had to grow up some time. And today was as good a time as any to begin.

———

"My mum was only saying this morning that she'd love to come over for supper again," improvised Chloë, casting a third desperate glance at the door to Jasmin's flat and wishing she would hurry up.

"Terrific!" beamed Jasmin's mother, who didn't look at all like someone with a guilty secret. "Alex dear, Chloë is Suzy Sanderson's daughter – you know, the TV presenter."

"You are?" Alex beamed at her. "Well, of course, I see it now – you have your mother's dazzling good looks, my dear."

Chloë flushed with pleasure and then reprimanded herself. She was supposed to be keeping an eye on this man, not being charmed by him.

"Well, Alex, you'd better be going!" Josephine got to her feet. "I have work to do and . . . oh, there you are Jasmin! Come to rescue Chloë from having to be polite to us oldies, have you?"

She turned to her visitor.

"Alex, this is my daughter, Jasmin. Jasmin, this is Alex Grainger. From the choir."

Flustered, Jasmin nodded, then grabbed Chloë's arm. "Come on, Chloë," she rushed, "let's go."

"Where . . ." her mother began.

"We're going to Chloë's," Jasmin improvised hastily. "To check some revision."

"You are?" Chloë looked aghast. "But . . ."

"You don't have to keep thanking me," said Jasmin brightly, stamping none too delicately on Chloë's toe. She dragged her to the door.

"Don't be long," called her mother. "I want you back here within the hour."

"You'll be back here long before that," hissed Chloë. "I've a romantic evening to prepare for."

"So," said Jasmin hopefully, "have I. Or at least a romantic twenty minutes. Now will you just get a move on. It's dark."

———

Nick pulled open the front door and turned to his mother. "I won't be long," he said. "I'm popping over to Chloë's to do some revision."

Jenny grinned. "Are you now?" she laughed. "You're quite sure it's revision you have in mind?"

"Mum!" objected Nick. "It's not like that . . ."

As he jogged up the street, he reflected that at least he knew now that it never would be. He wasn't going to waste any more time having adolescent fantasies about a girl who, nice though she was, would never think of him as anything other than a mate. In a way, it was a kind of relief; tonight, for example, he wouldn't have to think of witty one-liners, or wonder whether she fancied him. He would just play it straight, the way he did when he was with Sinead. Easy going, no stress.

As he turned the corner, he wondered for the second time in forty-eight hours, just what Sinead Flaherty was doing taking up permanent residence inside his head.

———

"And this college in London? You could actually go there and do your A levels and study animation, all at the same time?"

Jasmin perched next to Sanjay on the canal wall, leaning towards him in her excitement.

Sanjay nodded. "It's brilliant," he said. "There's an Art foundation course which runs in parallel with the A levels, so you get the best of both worlds. And a far better chance of getting a place on a Computer Visualisation and Animation course at uni."

"But doesn't it cost a bomb? I mean, with you having to board and everything."

Sanjay ploughed on enthusiastically. "It would do, yes," he agreed. "But Mr Lamport says there's this scholarship you can sit for. If you get it, all your fees are covered."

"Wow!" Jasmin looked impressed. "So go for it!"

"What?"

"Go for it," urged Jasmin. "I mean, you'd be crazy not to – it's your dream come true."

"Yes, but – it would mean leaving Lockbridge High at the end of next term."

For a moment Jasmin turned and gazed out over the

canal, images of school without Sanjay darting through her mind.

"Yes," she said briskly after a second or two. "But you can't do that same course anywhere up here, can you? And besides, you've got to go away some time, so why not now?"

Sanjay stared at her. This wasn't how he had imagined it would be. All the way over here, he had pictured her crumpling into floods of tears, pleading with him not to leave her. He had imagined taking her into his arms, stroking her hair, kissing her, holding her tight. And now here she was, urging him to go, making it sound as if it didn't matter to her one way or the other. How could she be like that?

"Oh well, great!" he burst out. "If that's all it matters to you . . ."

He jumped off the wall and began walking briskly towards the canal bridge.

"Sanjay! Wait!"

Jasmin ran after him. "What's the matter? What did I say?"

Sanjay turned. "You don't care, do you? It doesn't matter to you that I might go miles and miles away, that we might only get to see one another every few weeks. You couldn't care less!"

"Sanjay, that's not true, I do care . . ."

"Well, you have an odd way of showing it!"

Jasmin took Sanjay's hand. He snatched it away.

"Look, Sanjay," she said, struggling to keep the wobble out of her voice, "it's because I love you that I want you to go. Don't you see . . . ?"

"Oh yes, I see all right!" retorted Sanjay. "You've had enough of me and now you are ready to move on. Well, don't get your hopes up. The chances are I won't be going anywhere. For one thing, my father won't hear of it and for another, I probably don't stand a chance of winning the scholarship."

Jasmin stared at him, her eyes clouded. "Oh well," she said, "if you're going to take that attitude, you might as well accept defeat before you start. I thought you wanted to make animation your career; I thought art and design mattered to you. Clearly I was wrong."

"No," began Sanjay, "it does, but . . ."

"But, but, but!!" stormed Jasmin. "That's right – come up with a thousand excuses about why you can't ask your father, why you won't bother to sit the exam. OK, so he might say no; you might fail the exam. But if you don't try, you'll never know, will you? And then you'll spend the rest of your life wondering about what might have been. And I don't want that for you – get it? I don't want it because . . ." She faltered.

"Because what?" asked Sanjay softly.

"Because I love you," said Jasmin.

"But if you loved me, you would want me with you. If you told me that you were thinking of going away to college, I'd flip!"

"Would you?"

"Yes I would!"

"In that case," said Jasmin softly, "it's you who doesn't really love me." She took a deep breath and turned away.

"Where are you going?"

"Home," she said shortly.

"But – it's dark and . . ."

Jasmin turned and gave Sanjay a small smile. "Yes," she said. "But one day I'm going to have to go somewhere in the dark and there won't be anyone to hold my hand."

"Oh great – so you've made up your mind that I'm history, have you?"

Jasmin tried once more. "Sanjay, it's not like that . . ."

"Forget it!" Sanjay wheeled round and began walking away down the towpath. Jasmin swallowed.

She wanted to call him back, to say she was sorry, to beg him to walk her home.

But she couldn't. She wouldn't. Just as she knew that Sanjay had to give this college thing a go, so she knew she had to learn to overcome her terror on her own.

She took a deep breath and began walking back along the canalside. The curved Victorian streetlights spread pools of light over the cobbles. If she ran through the dark bits she could catch her breath when she got to each lamppost.

There was someone coming. Keep walking. Faster. Only two more blocks and you'll be there.

"Hi, Jasmin!"

She exhaled with relief. It was Nick.

"Hi!" she said. "Are you looking for your mum?"

Nick shook his head. "No," he replied. "I'm going round to Chloë's – homework."

I'll bet, thought Jasmin.

"See you tomorrow," called Nick with a wave.

"See you." She ran the last few yards to the café door. She had done it. She had walked home in the dark. OK, so it was only five hundred metres, but it was a start.

She was just sorry that to do it, she had had to have a row with Sanjay.

————

"So, have we all had a good day?" Sanjay's father glanced round the dinner table.

"I have," announced Rani. "I got a star."

"Well done!" exclaimed Sanjay's mother. "What for?"

"Going to the shop and getting the right things and the right change," said Rani proudly. "All by myself, without any help at all."

"Brilliant!" Sanjay smiled at her. For most twelve-year-olds, shopping was a doddle; for Rani, who had Down's syndrome, working out her money and remembering what she needed to buy was a big achievement. He was dead proud of her.

"And you, Sanjay?" his father queried.

Sanjay swallowed. "Well," he began. "Actually, I went to see . . ."

"It's no good!" His mother suddenly jumped up from the table, clapping her hands. "I can't wait a moment longer. If I don't tell you, I shall burst!"

"Tell us what?" her husband asked. "You haven't landed that post at Durham, have you?"

Dipti shook her head impatiently. "No," she said. "Better than that."

"What, Mum?" Sanjay leaned forward.

"My book," declared his mother. "Gardner and Evans are going to publish my book."

"WOW!" Sanjay jumped up and hugged his mum. "You mean the romantic novel? That one?"

His mother had written so many boring academic books over the years but this was something else.

His mum nodded enthusiastically. "And there's more," she said. "They want a sequel. They are commissioning me to write another one. With money up front."

"Brilliant!" cried Sanjay. "Isn't that great, Dad?"

Mr Fraser dabbed his mouth with his napkin and looked at his wife. "Dipti," he said, "are you telling me that people are actually prepared to pay you for writing that sort of banal rubbish?"

All the joy went from Mrs Fraser's face. She sat down and began toying with her chicken. "You haven't read it," she said softly. "If you did, you might be quite proud of me."

"Oh my dear," said Duncan hastily, "I am proud of you. I'm proud of your achievements in the fields of research, I'm proud of the books you have written on Hindu mythology, on life in rural Rajasthan . . ."

"But not," concluded Dipti, "proud of me because I've written what thousands more people will read and enjoy, I suppose."

"It seems such a waste of your talents, that's all," sighed her husband. "Rather like Sanjay here wanting to spend his life drawing cartoons when he has the brain to become a top lawyer."

Sanjay's heart sank. There was no point telling his father about Mr Lamport's idea now. He would only ridicule the whole thing.

He would wait. Get his mum to have a word. After all, he had until Friday.

There was no point making waves. Whatever Jasmin said.

Chapter 8

A CHANGE OF PLAN

CHLOË looked at her reflection in the long mirror on her bedroom wall and nodded in satisfaction. She looked cool. Her pale pink skirt was short enough to be alluring but long enough not to be tarty; her nail polish exactly matched her lilac vest top and her new suede clogs made her legs look at least four centimetres longer.

In short, she thought, unscrewing her mascara wand and peering into the mirror, the overall look was one of cool sophistication.

"Suzy! Chloë! Where are you?"

Chloë jumped, smudging mascara on her cheek as she ran to the door. Dad! He was back! But he was meant to be in Glasgow overnight.

"Edward? Darling, what a lovely surprise!"

Suzy's mother was running down the stairs, a bright smile on her lips. Only Chloë, after years of practice, noticed the tension in her shoulders, the way her throat was working and her hands clenching and unclenching as she approached her husband.

"What are you doing back . . . ?"

"Meeting cancelled," he said airily. "Get your coats, you two! We're going out on the town!"

His black mood had vanished. His eyes were laughing, and from behind his back he produced a huge bunch of freesias which he handed to Suzy, planting a kiss on her cheek as he did so.

"Edward, they're lovely!" Suzy cried. "I'll just get a vase . . ."

"Later, later!" cried Edward, who was almost manic with excitement. "Come on – I've a table booked at La Pergola for seven thirty."

He glanced up the stairs to where Chloë was standing. "You look terrific, angel," he called. "But hurry – it's hell to park in the city at this time of night."

Chloë looked at her mum, who nodded encouragingly.

"I can't come, Dad," ventured Chloë. "I've got . . ."

She saw the pleading look in her mother's eyes and faltered.

"Can't come?" riposted Edward. "Nonsense. I know it's a school night but so what? If we can't have a family night out once in a while . . ."

So that was it. Of course, thought Chloë, I should have realised. It was always the same. He'd hit her mum, storm out of the house and then suddenly want to play happy families, always choosing some crowded restaurant where he would know heaps of people. All evening he would be stroking Suzy's arm, adjusting her chair, buying her drinks – in short, playing the perfect husband.

Just thinking about it made Chloë feel sick. "No, Dad," she said. "The thing is, I've got a mate coming round and . . ."

Edward's face lost its smile. "And your mates are more important than your parents . . ." he began.

"Of course they're not, are they, darling?" This time Chloë could not ignore the pleading tone in her mother's voice. "Just give Nick a ring and grab your coat, there's a love."

Suzy's eyes met Chloë's and Chloë knew she had to go. If she didn't, her dad would start on his old routine of telling Mum that she was a lousy parent, that Chloë had far too much attitude for a teenager and that it was all her fault for spending more time being a media personality than a proper mother.

"OK," she said, as brightly as she could. "Won't be a minute."

"This is so lovely of you, Edward," she heard her mother say as she picked up the extension phone to dial Nick's number.

"I want to make it up to you, Suzy," her father replied. "I didn't mean . . ."

Chloë slammed the bedroom door shut. She didn't want to hear it – those same, meaningless words, those empty promises, those shallow excuses. How could her mum stand there, all smiles and false excitement when she knew – absolutely knew – that within a few weeks she'd be bruised and bleeding again? Chloë loved her mum but there were times, and this was one of them, when she wanted to grab her by the shoulders and shake her . . . no! Chloë gasped. She was thinking like her father. She could never hurt her mum. But somehow, she wished there was a way to make her see what was happening to her. To all of them.

"Sugar!" She slammed the receiver down. Engaged. Get off the phone, Nick!

"Chloë!" Her father's voice was tinged with impatience.

"Coming!"

Hurriedly she redialled. Engaged. It was no good. She would have to go. Why did this have to happen tonight? Just when she was really getting somewhere with Nick.

But there would be other nights. And after this disappointment, he'd be even more anxious to spend time with her. In fact, it might work to her advantage. It didn't do to be too available.

As she brushed past her desk, her eye fell on her Geography homework. It had to be in tomorrow.

Still, she would just have to set the alarm and do it in the morning. Right now, keeping the peace at home was the major priority.

As always.

———

Jasmin held the receiver close to her mouth and willed her mother not to appear.

"Mrs Fraser? Hi, it's Jasmin. Is Sanjay there? Thanks."

She waited, chewing her lip and willing her heart to stop pounding.

"Hello?"

"Hi, Sanjay, it's me. Look, about tonight . . ."

"I'm sorry." Sanjay sounded relieved to hear her voice. "I just love you so much and . . ."

"I love you too," whispered Jasmin. "That's why I want you to be happy, whatever it takes. I'll always be here for you, Sanjay, always."

"Really?"

"Really. Now what are you doing tonight?"

Sanjay sighed. "Maths, Biology, German . . ."

"Not that, silly," laughed Jasmin. "You're going to tell your dad about the scholarship."

"I am?"

"Yes, you are," said Jasmin firmly. "Do you love me?"

"I just said . . ."

"Then do it. For me. OK?"

"OK."

Jasmin replaced the receiver and slumped down on to the chair. London. It was miles away. What if he got the scholarship? What if he went and met loads of other girls – wittier, prettier, all clued up about computers and design and stuff?

She could feel tears pricking behind her eyes.

Perhaps she should have begged him to stay after all. If he went, her life was going to be so empty.

But if he didn't, his might be. And she couldn't bear that for him.

They'd find a way. True love always did.

Didn't it?

———

Nick rang the Sandersons' doorbell for the third time. No reply. Terrific, he thought. She could at least have phoned to tell me she had had a better offer. Not that it mattered, of course; it wasn't as if they were an item or anything. If she'd gone out with someone else, so what? Good luck to her.

He turned and headed down the stairs. What a waste of half an evening! By the time he got home it would hardly be worth settling down to work before he had to stop to watch 'Red Dwarf' and . . .

"Mum, it's only a Science book, for heaven's sake! I'll borrow Chloë's, OK?"

Nick stopped dead on the stairs and peered up to the half landing as a door slammed, followed by thundering footsteps and a lot of muttering.

"Honestly, mothers! All that aggro over a lost book! Neurotic or what?"

Sinead careered towards him, hair flying and forehead puckered in an angry frown. She looked, Nick thought, dead cute.

"Hey!" he called. "Training for the Apartment Block one hundred-metre dash, are you?"

Sinead wheeled round, her mouth dropping open in amazement as she saw Nick. "Nick!" The word came out as a strangled gasp.

"Hi!" he said. "You look like you're fleeing from a herd of rampant elephants!"

Her face broke into a grin. She seemed, thought Nick, very breathless for someone who had only sprinted down one short corridor.

"No," she said. "Just one over-stressed mother who seems to think that the future of the universe depends on me getting an A-grade for GCSE Chemistry. As if!"

She leaned against the bannister. "So what are you doing here?"

"Well, I was coming to see . . ."

He paused. And cleared his throat. ". . . you, actually."

Why did I say that? he asked himself. Because, he replied firmly to the voice in his head, you don't want to look like a total dork who has been stood up by Chloë Sanderson.

"Me?" Sinead's face broke into a broad grin. "Really? What for?"

Nick grinned. "You mean, aside from your sparkling wit and biting intellect?"

Sinead giggled. "And my secret supply of Walnut Whips!"

"That too," smiled Nick, and gave a mock sigh of

despair. The fact is, you are the only person I know who is actually turned on by rift valleys and glacial deposits. Could we do this Geography thing together?"

Sinead stared at him and Nick noticed a rather delightful little pink flush creeping slowly but surely up her neck.

"Unless, of course," he said hastily, "you've got better things to do. Which you probably have – seeing as how I didn't phone or . . ."

"No," smiled Sinead. "I've nothing better to do. Nothing at all. Come and have some ice cream."

"Ice cream?"

"It is an unwritten law that you can't produce good essays without a substantial intake of Double Chocolate Chip with added sprinkles."

Nick burst out laughing and followed her to the door of her apartment. As he did so, a car door slammed down in the courtyard below. It occurred to him that it could be Chloë arriving home.

But he didn't think he would bother to find out.

Chapter 9

CRISIS UPON CRISIS

BY THE last period on Tuesday, Chloë was distinctly annoyed. For one thing, she had slept through her alarm and failed to hand in her Geography essay and Mrs Littlebury had gone totally over the top and accused her of a lackadaisical approach to her work. But what was worse was the fact that Nick had not seemed the least bit fazed by finding her out the previous evening.

"Oh, don't worry," he had said airily when she apologised. "These things happen. I went to Sinead's instead and we . . ."

"You went where?"

"Sinead's," he said. "She's brilliant at Geography."

Oh, is she? thought Chloë. Keep calm. Remember, cool sophistication.

"So how about tonight?" she had invited him. "I've got the new In the Mould CD and . . ."

Nick had shaken his head. "Sorry," he said. "I've done

the Geography so there's no point really."

Chloë had been speechless, which for her was something of a new experience.

"I don't believe it!" she moaned to Jasmin on the way home. "I mean, I know he fancies me . . ."

"Maybe he's moved on," suggested Jasmin. "Given up. After all, it was a bit off, you standing him up last night."

"I couldn't help it, I had to . . ."

"Go out with Mummy and Daddy – I know," sighed Jasmin. "You should have refused. You should have stood your ground and told them straight and . . ."

"What the hell do you know about anything?"

Chloë shouted so loudly that several kids on the bus turned to gawp at her. "You haven't a clue what it's like – you with your oh-so-lovey-dovey family . . ."

"Oh sure!" It was Jasmin's turn to get aerated. "A mother who is . . ."

She dropped her voice. ". . . carrying on with some guy from choir. And a dad who is so taken up with gutting a battered barge that he can't see how much she's changed and . . ."

Chloë reached out and squeezed her hand. "Sorry," she said. "Really. But at least you don't have to spend every day worrying . . ."

She stopped, horrified at how close she had come to saying too much.

"Worrying about what?"

Chloë smiled. "Nothing," she said. "I'm being stupid. I'm due on – take no notice of me."

Jasmin nodded sympathetically because she knew that was what Chloë expected. But she wasn't daft. She knew full well that there was far more to her friend's outburst than a three-week long dose of PMT. And she had a feeling that it wasn't all down to Nick Bowen either.

———

By Wednesday night, Sinead was in seventh heaven. Not only had her evening with Nick been the stuff of which dreams are made, but for the past two days he had sat with her at lunch-time and spent every break chatting to her, telling her she was funny and wacky and a real laugh. OK, so sophisticated, sexy and dead alluring would have been better but the fact was that Nick was with her and not Chloë – and as miracles went that had to rate a Perfect Ten.

Sadly things weren't quite so ideal at home. For a start, her dad had given her mum this mega-huge pack of vitamins for the over fifties and her mum was only forty-seven, which went down a bundle. And then he had told her that he had some great news that would cheer her up, only it seemed to have had the opposite effect.

"This mate of Declan's has placed a huge order," he had told them over breakfast. "Six tables, twenty-four chairs and a matching sideboard, all to be decorated with figures from Irish folk legends. For some classy restaurant he's opening in Liverpool."

"Nice," murmured Kathleen.

"Isn't it?" agreed Shaun, encouraged. "That'll make up for those wardrobes Fred Baxter never paid for . . ."

Sinead could see that the moment the words had slipped out, her father regretted opening his mouth.

"Never paid for?" her mother had shouted. "You mean you shelled out for the stuff and spent all that time and . . ."

"Fred'll pay, soon enough," said Shaun. "He's just having a bit of a sticky patch with the hotel right now."

Kathleen had whipped his copy of *The Racing Post* from his hands. "And it's sticky patches we'll be having if you waste time on this rubbish," she retorted. "Horses, indeed! The money situation's not good, you know."

Sinead's dad had laughed. "Don't be daft," he said. "There's loads sloshing around."

"Oh is there?" replied Kathleen. "After we bought this place, we set aside one hundred and fifty thousand of that inheritance to spend, remember?"

"Yes, and . . ."

"And what with all the new furniture for this place and holidays, your business, that horse and that daft new car of yours, most of it's gone. The rest's invested, remember? For capital growth."

Shaun had fidgeted in discomfort. Sinead knew from her primary school days that figures terrified her father.

"So don't be thinking everything's a bed of roses because it's not," concluded Kathleen.

She stood up, sniffing loudly. "And now I'm off – taking my cherubs swimming."

Her voice had softened, the way it always did when she referred to the special needs kids she worked with at Downside School.

"Rani too?" asked Sinead, who had a soft spot for Sanjay's sister.

"Sure," her mum had replied. "Terrified of water she is, bless her – but we'll get her there. Mind you . . ."

"What?"

"I can't go till I've polished this table – look, finger marks." An expression of real worry had crossed Kathleen's face.

"I'll do it," Sinead had offered hurriedly, anxious to hang on to her mother's good mood. "I haven't got to leave for ten minutes. You get ready."

Her mum had looked doubtful. "Well, I . . ."

"Go on, Mum. I'll do it, OK?"

"You're not usually this helpful," her mother had commented.

"It's usually me that does the jobs," added Erin smugly.

"Well, today it's me," Sinead had said airily, refusing even to rise to her sister's bait. It was so very easy, she reflected now, to be nice to the entire universe when you were passionately, totally and irrevocably in love.

By Thursday evening, Sanjay knew he couldn't avoid the issue any longer. Mr Lamport had been getting more and more impatient for an answer and Jasmin had told him categorically that if he didn't tell his dad about the scholarship this evening, she would personally turn up on the doorstep and deal with it herself. A week ago he would have laughed at such an idea; now he had no doubt that she meant it.

He had taken the first steps; he had told his mum, and asked her to have a word with his father. But she had been dashing off to London to see her publishers and sign contracts and eat dinner in posh restaurants and had told him it was down to him.

"I'm so thrilled for you, darling," she had told him, while rifling through her selection of saris for something suitable for L'Escargot in Soho. "You must go for it."

"But what about Dad? Couldn't you just . . . ?"

She had placed her hands firmly on his shoulders. "No, Sanjay," she had said. "You're a great guy but it's time you stopped sitting on the fence. If Dad blows his top, then you just keep your cool, give him the facts and say that this is your life and you have to live it your way. I'll support you."

She paused to peer in the mirror at her new hairstyle. "But remember," she added, "it does no harm to meet him halfway. Right?"

"Right!" At the time, Sanjay had told himself he could do it. Now, sitting at the dining-table opposite his father and picking at a plate of salad, he wasn't so sure.

"Dad?"

"Yes?"

"Mr Lamport called me into his study the other day – and gave me this." He thrust the college brochure across the table.

"Beckendon College," read his father. "A centre for excellence with an eye to the future." He began flicking through the pages.

"There's a course, Dad – it's A levels – all the ones you want me to do – but you can take an Art foundation course at the same time and that means you stand a much better chance of getting into Bournemouth University to . . ."

"BOURNEMOUTH?" His father made it sound as if Sanjay had suggested completing his education on a small Pacific atoll.

"That's where the National Centre for Computer Animation is," muttered Sanjay.

Duncan laid down his knife and fork and gazed at him.

Here it comes, thought Sanjay miserably. No son of mine . . . wasting your brain . . . the Frasers have all been academics . . . It's Oxbridge for you, my boy . . .

He wondered which line his father would take this time.

"You really want to do this, don't you, son?"

Sanjay was astonished at the gentleness in his dad's voice.

"Yes I do. Very much."

His father nodded. "I don't suppose you've given a thought to the cost?"

Sanjay thrust another piece of paper at him. "Yes – see, there's this scholarship. Mr Lamport thinks I have a chance."

His father scanned the paper. "The Louis Breançon Scholarship – good heavens above!"

Sanjay's heart which had lifted slightly, sank.

"Louis Breançon – he's Felix Hadland's father-in-law."

Sanjay wondered what that had to do with anything and then remembered that Felix was the professor who had come to supper the week before.

Things suddenly began to fall into place.

"Great guy – met him when he lectured at Edinburgh last year. Well, well. So he's funded this thing."

Sanjay waited while his dad flicked through the prospectus.

" '. . . course designed to develop an interdisciplinary culture that transcends the art/science divide . . .' Sounds reasonable '. . . develops creative design skills in tandem with mathematics . . .' Indeed? Fascinating."

Sanjay held his breath.

"Well . . ." Duncan closed the booklet.

Sanjay's heart pounded.

". . . I don't want to be a wet blanket but, whatever Felix thinks, it's a jungle out there and . . ."

What was it his mum had said? Meet him halfway. "So if I do the A levels you suggested – Maths, Computer studies, History . . ."

"Alongside this Art foundation thing, you mean?"

Sanjay nodded. ". . . then if I mess up with the animation idea, I'll still have the right qualifications for another degree, won't I?"

"OK," said his dad.

"Pardon? You mean . . ."

His dad smiled. "I'm not over the moon about it," he said. "But I've done a lot of thinking and if you're dead set on it . . ."

"I am."

"Then go for it!" his dad concluded. "Mind you, if you don't get the scholarship, there's no way your mother and I could afford . . ."

"No, I know that, Dad!" Sanjay jumped up and hugged his father. Duncan looked incredibly surprised and rather pleased.

"I think we had better go and take a look at this college," said his dad. "That suit you?"

"Oh wow!"

"I take it," grinned Duncan, "that means yes."

———

"No, Sanjay, I'm afraid Jasmin can't come to the phone right now . . . come over? No, dear. I'm sorry. Goodbye!"

Jasmin caught the end of her mother's abrupt conversation as she came into the kitchen. "MUM!" She grabbed her mother's arm. "Was that Sanjay?"

"It was," said her mother. "He wanted to see you."

"And?"

"And I said no," said her mother.

"That is just so typical of you!" Jasmin shouted. "You go on and on about respect, and then you show me none at all!"

Her mother raised her immaculately plucked eyebrows heavenwards and sighed. "Jasmin, do we have to go through all this yet again? You know the rules – on school nights you stay in and work, at weekends you go out. You've got GCSEs coming up, if you remember."

"Remember?" spat Jasmin, raising her voice above the clattering of dishes. "As if I could ever forget, the way you keep going on at me! Don't you realise that parental pressure is a major cause of teenage stress? I read it in a newspaper."

Her mother scooped up some dirty glasses and headed for the dishwasher. "Oh really?" she replied, clearly unimpressed by the information.

"Yes, really," began Jasmin. "It said that kids can be psychologically damaged and what's more . . ."

"Jasmin, I don't have the time to hang about arguing with you," interrupted Josephine emphatically. "These exams are crucial for your future and . . ."

"Oh right!! So from now until June the twelfth I'm supposed to become a hermit, am I? Besides, it's not like I'm going out to rave all night. All my other friends are allowed to visit one another whenever they want."

"Well you're not, OK?" snapped her mother, slamming the door of the dishwasher with unnecessary force and ignoring the look of surprise of Anton, the underchef. "A fat lot of book work you'd do, mooning about round at that boy's place."

Jasmin gasped in disbelief. "Oh I get it! It's not really about work, is it? It's about Sanjay. It's about the fact that you are narrow-minded, bigoted, prejudiced . . ."

"Jasmin!" Her mother wheeled round, her dark eyes flashing a warning as Anton almost dropped the fish he was gutting. "I have taken about as much as I am prepared to take. It has nothing to do with Sanjay. I just don't think . . ."

"You don't think I should be seeing an Asian guy, right? You only want me to have African-Caribbean boyfriends . . ."

"I don't particularly want you to have a boyfriend at all at the moment!" her mother retorted and then closed her eyes, sighing deeply as she realised her very obvious mistake.

"Precisely! That just goes to prove my point!" stormed Jasmin. "You treat me like a kid."

"Which considering you are behaving like one . . ."

"And you're not exactly saintly yourself, are you?"

Her mother stared at her. "What do you mean?"

"I've seen you, sidling off with . . ."

The door flew open and Jasmin's dad burst in. "It's come!" He was waving a sheet of paper above his head.

"What has?" asked Josie.

"The licence to convert the boat into a floating cocktail

bar!" he cried. "Now we can begin working on it."

"We?" queried his wife.

"Of course we," he cried. "We're in this together, aren't we?"

Mrs Johnson smiled and patted his arm. "Yes, love," she said. "Of course we are."

"Exciting, isn't it?" cried Harry.

"Very," said Mrs Johnson. The words, thought Jasmin, were right. The expression on her mother's face, however, was quite wrong.

Chapter 10

HOPES, FEARS AND BRIBERY

"BUT SIR, I can't! I mean, that's impossible!"

Sanjay looked aghast at the headmaster, who waggled a finger at him in mock severity. "Nothing's impossible, Sanjay, if you make up your mind to do it," he said. "Your interview is on Monday at twelve noon – the day before we break up for Easter. Be there!"

Sanjay gulped. Monday? But today was Friday! In the ten days since his dad had agreed to let him apply for the scholarship he had worked his socks off, bringing his portfolio up to date, staying late after school for Mr Buckley to give him pointers on how to impress the lecturers – but somehow, none of it had seemed for real. Now the head was telling him that in just three days' time he had to get a train to London and face a whole load of strangers who would probably think he was totally up himself for imagining for one second that he could ever make the grade.

"They combine the interviews with Open Day," the headmaster was saying, "so you'll be able to get a real feel for the place. Give your parents a chance to take a look too."

As he ambled back to his classroom, Sanjay found himself pausing to look into rooms he had seen a zillion times before. The Biology lab where he'd almost fainted at the sight of a dead frog when he was in Year Seven; the library where he'd hidden during PE lessons, preferring to read cartoon books and practise his drawing than to do press-ups on a cold gymnasium floor; the Art cupboard where he and Jasmin had kissed one day when everything seemed to be against them.

He would miss it. A lot. He'd never thought about the reality of it before; he'd just taken the place for granted.

You're crazy, he told himself firmly. You're talking as if it is all cut and dried. Get real. There are going to be dozens of kids after this scholarship. Chances are you'll still be here in two years' time.

Far from making him despondent, he actually found the thought quite comforting.

———

"Nick! Wait!" Chloë raised her voice above the babble in the canteen and waved an arm to attract his attention.

With satisfaction she saw him turn to Sinead and then head across towards the vacant space at Chloë's table. This was it. This time she knew she was on to a winner. Never mind spending an evening doing boring homework – she was going to have a whole day away from Leeds with Nick – just him and her. OK, and a couple of thousand other people.

"So," she said brightly as Nick sat down beside her, "do you want the good news or the mega-amazing brilliant news?"

Nick eyed her quizzically.

"Well?"

"OK – the good news," he said.

"There's a sports exhibition on in Bradford during the Easter holidays," she said.

Nick nodded. "I know," he said. "It's huge – they've got all these extreme sports as well as footie and cricket and stuff. I was reading about it – it's dead expensive, though."

"Now do you want the mega-amazing brilliant bit?" Chloë parted her lips slightly and let her tongue caress her two front teeth for a second.

"Which is?"

Chloë paused for a moment, to make sure she had his full attention. "Ta-ra!" she said, and with a flourish planted two tickets on the table.

"What's that?"

To Chloë's intense annoyance, Sinead had spotted a free space at the table and was already settling herself down.

"Go on," urged Chloë, totally ignoring her and grinning at Nick. "Read what it says."

Nick fingered the tickets, his eyes widening in amazement. *"VIP Pass – MegaSport UK – Press Day April 5th,"* he read. "Chloë, you're a miracle worker!"

"One aims to please," she said coyly. "Actually, my mum got them through the TV show – loads of celebs will be there. She's interviewed half of them. So are you up for it?"

"I'll say!" beamed Nick. "Try keeping me away."

Oh I won't be doing that, thought Chloë.

"You'll come, won't you, Sinead?" Nick asked, shoving one of the tickets under her nose.

"She can't come!" expostulated Chloë before Sinead had the chance to reply. "There are only two tickets!"

"No, look," said Nick calmly. "Each one says *Admit Two.* So that means four of us can go."

"What?" Chloë spat out the question and snatched one of the tickets from Nick's hand. He was right. How could she have been so dumb? Why hadn't she read the tickets properly? And more importantly, how was she going to make sure that Sinead didn't muscle in on her special day out?

"Well, I – er, I guess it's not really your thing, Sinead," she babbled. "I mean, it's all dry ski slopes . . ."

"Oh cool," said Sinead. "I've always wanted to try that."

". . . and in-line skating and real tennis and . . ."

"Ace!" grinned Sinead. "But Chloë . . . ?"

"Yes?"

"I didn't think you were into sport and stuff," said Sinead sweetly. "Didn't you say during the five-a-side tournament that you would rather be watching paint dry?"

She stood up without waiting for a reply. "Anyway, thank your mum for me, won't you?" she smiled. "It's going to be a brilliant day."

Oh sure, thought Chloë miserably. Absolutely great with you coming along to play gooseberry.

What worried her most as she dragged herself along to afternoon registration was the possibility that it might not be Sinead who was the odd one out.

———

"So you see, you have to come!" Chloë poked Jasmin's arm to keep her attention.

"No way," shuddered Jasmin. "It's not my scene."

"But you have to come," insisted Chloë. "I need you there. If you come, you can take Sinead off somewhere, and leave me alone with Nick."

"Get real!" protested Jasmin. "Anyway, I don't know what you're worrying about – it's ages away yet."

"Two weeks," said Chloë. "So?"

"So Sinead might get flu, you might break a leg, Nick might meet someone else . . ."

"Oh thanks!"

"All I'm saying," continued Jasmin, "is play it cool. Go with the flow. Getting screwed up about it won't help."

"Well, that's rich, coming from you," interjected Chloë.

"You weren't exactly calm personified about your mum and that Alex guy – what happened about them, anyway?"

Jasmin pursed her lips.

"He calls for her every time she goes to choir practice," she replied, "and last night, I answered the phone and the line went dead."

"And you think it was him?"

"I don't know what else to think!" cried Jasmin.

"Look, it really doesn't sound to me as if there's anything going on," said Chloë reassuringly. "But if it's really worrying you, why don't you speak to your mum?"

Jasmin dropped her eyes. "I want to," she said, "and then again, I don't. For as long as I don't ask the question . . ."

". . . you won't have to face up to the answer," concluded Chloë.

Jasmin nodded. "I mean, what if she admits it? What if she's planning to go off with him? What if . . . ?"

"Hang on!" Chloë touched her arm. "You're letting your imagination run away with you. You don't know anything's happening. And even if they are having a bit of a thing, your mum would never leave your dad – or you, for that matter."

She saw the anxiety in Jasmin's eyes and quickly squeezed her hand. "Don't worry," she said. "It's not as if your mum's got any reason to go. I mean, she's not having to put up with . . ."

What was she saying?

"Put up with what?"

"Nothing," said Chloë hastily. "Gosh, is that the time?" She grabbed her books and headed off hurriedly towards the Science block.

"Chloë, wait!"

Don't ask me what I meant, Chloë willed her silently. Don't.

"I'll come to the sports thing with you if you like," said Jasmin.

Chloë stopped dead and seized her arms. "You will? Oh, that's great. Thanks a million."

"I can't promise it'll work," warned Jasmin.

"Oh, it will work," declared Chloë. "It has to work. Something has got to go right in my life."

As they parted company at the foot of the stairs, Jasmin wondered, not for the first time, just what it was that was wrong with Chloë's seemingly idyllic existence.

———

While Chloë was hastily covering her tracks, her mum was sitting in Nathan Reed's production office at Pennine TV.

"No, Nathan, for the very last time, I will not do it!" she declared. "I've never refused an interview before but this one is a non-starter."

Nathan shook his head and looked puzzled. "But Suzy," he pleaded, "Isla Idris is the top box office draw of the decade – you know that, I know that. And she's offering us an exclusive – an insight into this new role of hers and . . ."

"Nathan!" Suzy's voice rose an octave as she stood up and headed for the door. "Read my lips! The answer is NO!"

She pulled open the door and ran out of the office and down the corridor. She knew that Nathan was expecting her to explain why she had refused, but of course, there was no way she could do that. It was out of the question. Just as conducting a live interview on morning TV with Isla Idris was out of the question.

Suzy knew what the film was about. Suzy knew the questions she would be forced to ask. And no matter how much of a professional she might be, there were some things even she could never, ever do.

"Well," said Nick as he and Sinead headed for the school bus, "what shall we do tomorrow night?"

Sinead swallowed. Did he mean 'we' as in the gang, or 'we' as in him and her? Together. On their own.

"Well," she ventured, "Jasmin and Sanjay were talking about going bowling . . ."

"I don't want to go with Jasmin and Sanjay, I want to go with you," said Nick. "Unless, of course, you have other plans."

"Well," said Sinead thoughtfully. "I don't know."

Nick wondered why he suddenly felt so desperately disappointed.

"See, I will have to phone Brad Pitt and cancel," said Sinead with a twinkle in her eye, "and I know Leo di

Caprio will be mortified, but . . . yes, I think I can fit you in!"

Nick's face broke into a broad grin. "Cool," he said. "How about supper at Mario's?"

Sinead opened her mouth and not one sound came out.

"I know what you are going to say," added Nick. "Revision."

Sinead shook her head. "Stuff revision," she said. "What time?"

Chapter 11

FANNING THE FLAMES

NICK was surprised at just how much he was looking forward to the evening. It was great going out with the gang, but tonight he'd have Sinead all to himself. He knew they would have a real laugh and talk about everything under the sun – and maybe . . .

He ran his fingers through his gelled hair, his hands shaking just a little. This was crazy – Sinead was just a mate. And that's all he wanted right now. Unless . . .

The insistent shrilling of the doorbell shattered the rather romantic image that had somehow infiltrated his imagination. Spot on time – good old Sinead! Grabbing his wallet and spraying a final jet of Rugged aftershave, just for good measure, he sped down the stairs two at a time.

"It's OK, Mum, I'll get it!" he called but his mother was already opening the door.

"Bullseye! You must be Jenny Bowen!"

Nick stopped dead in his tracks, his hand gripping the bannister. There, in the rain, was Mike Lovell. And there wasn't a thing he could do about it.

"Yes?" Jenny's voice held a questioning note.

"Mike Lovell." The guy held out a hand. "You probably won't remember me – mate of Greg's from way back!"

"Yes, my mother told me . . ." Nick's mother sounded hesitant.

"If you knew the trouble I've had tracking you down," he continued. "Anyone would think you'd gone into hiding!" He roared with laughter.

"But I'm not one to give up easily, and here I am. So where is he, the old rogue?"

Jenny gripped the doorknob and a small shudder shook her slight frame. Nick bounded down the last eight steps.

"How dare you . . ."

Mike turned, his eyes widening in recognition. "Well!" he exclaimed. "The guy who swore blind that no Bowen lived here!"

There was a look of reproof in his eyes which really got Nick going. "Actually," he retorted, "I never said that and anyway, how dare you come here, upsetting my mother, talking about my father as if he was still . . ."

"NICK!" His mother's voice held a note of warning. "It's all right."

She swallowed and then looked up at Mike. "Mr

Lovell," she said calmly, "I think you had better come in. There is clearly a lot you don't know."

———

Some Saturday night this was turning out to be, thought Chloë miserably. Seven fifteen and still no plans. She'd phoned Nick but he said he was tied up, and Jasmin was spending the evening psyching up Sanjay for his interview.

Which just left Sinead.

Not that Sinead was her favourite person right now. But she was fun – and of course, if Chloë was with her she couldn't be on the phone to Nick, could she?

She would pop downstairs and ask her up to listen to music or watch a video. And at the same time, she could warn her off Nick – nicely, of course. For her own good. To prevent her from being devastated later.

That's what she would do.

Anything was better than another evening alone with her thoughts.

———

"DEAD?" Mike Lovell's face drained of colour. "Greg? But he can't – I mean, when? How?"

Nick saw his mother bite her lip and quickly intervened. "My dad had a heart attack," he said rapidly. "He was up a ladder, pruning a tree and . . ."

At that moment there was an impatient knocking on the front door followed by a loud ring of the bell.

Nick leaped up. Sinead! He couldn't let her come in on

all this – not with this guy about to start on about money owing and commitments to be met. But he couldn't just go out and leave his mum to face the music alone.

He dashed into the hall and opened the door.

"Hi!" Sinead was standing on the step, rain dripping off the end of her nose.

"Hi – look, I'm really sorry, something's cropped up and . . ."

"What?" Her face fell.

"It's just that – well, I can't ask you in because . . ."

The kitchen door banged behind him. "Good gracious, Nick, don't stand there chattering," cried his grandmother. "Your friend will catch her death. Hello, you must be Sinead. In you come, love."

"No, I . . ." Nick began.

But Sinead was in.

"I'm just taking tea through to your mum and that nice Mr Lovell," chatted his gran. "Want a cup, Sinead?"

"No, she doesn't," interrupted Nick as his grandmother opened the door.

"So you'd better tell me here and now just how much it is my husband owed you," Jenny's voice was clear and unwavering, "because that's what you've come for, Mr Lovell, isn't it? Money?"

Nick kicked out a foot and the door slammed closed. "Let's go!" he said hastily, pushing Sinead down the hall.

"But I thought you said you couldn't," she reasoned. "I don't mind staying in if you . . ."

"NO!" Nick's voice brooked no argument.

Sinead merely nodded and followed him out into the street, pulling up her collar against the driving rain.

This time Nick didn't take her hand. He plunged his hands deep into his jacket pockets and, head down, began walking down the road.

Sinead knew better than to say a word. She merely fell in step beside him and stayed silent.

———

Chloë rang the doorbell of the Flahertys' flat for the second time. It played the first few bars of 'Land of Hope and Glory', which Chloë thought was incredibly naff.

Slowly the door opened a chink, held by a chain.

Erin's pale face peeped out and then relaxed into a grin of relief. "Oh, it's you, Chloë!" she said. "I thought it might be a burglar."

"Burglars don't usually knock first," laughed Chloë. "Is Sinead in?"

Erin shook her head. "Nope," she said. "She's out on the pull."

Chloë's eyes widened. Sinead's little sister was not known for her street language – or for knowing anything about boys, for that matter.

"Come in." Erin opened the door wide and stepped back. "Mum and Dad are out too – hence the chain. They won't be long . . ."

"On the pull with who?" demanded Chloë.

"Whom," said Erin.

"Excuse me?"

"It's with whom, not with who," declared Erin. "Grammar."

Sinead's right, thought Chloë dryly. A right prissy little madam.

"She's with that Nick guy," said Erin calmly. "You know, the one who captained the five-a-side . . ."

"I know which one!" retorted Chloë. So that was why he said he was tied up. He was with her. How could he? How dare she?

"So did you want to tell her something? Shall I give her a message?"

Chloë bit her lip. "No, it's fine," she said. "I've plenty to tell her, but I'll do it myself. Thanks."

"You're jealous," observed Erin. "Sinead said you . . . oh sugar!"

The doorbell rang, and Erin scuttled to open the door.

"Mr Flaherty at home?"

Erin looked terrified. Standing in the doorway were two police officers, twiddling their caps in their hands.

"What? No. Why? What's happened?"

"Mrs Flaherty, then?"

Erin shook her head and looked close to tears.

"I'm Chloë Sanderson and I live in the flat upstairs," Chloë intervened. "Can I help?"

The police officer looked doubtful. "Not really," he said.

"It's Sinead, isn't it?" Erin burst into tears. "She's been run over, mugged . . ."

The policewoman stepped forward. "Nothing's happened to any of your family," she said reassuringly. "But we need to speak to Mr Flaherty urgently. It's about his workshop. It's gone up in flames."

———

"What's that you're reading?" Edward Sanderson strode into the sitting-room and gestured at the sheaf of papers in Suzy's hands.

"This?" Suzy looked up in alarm. "Oh nothing – just the minutes of the last production meeting."

She stuffed the papers hastily into her bag and turned to Edward.

"So – new projects – more promotions in the pipeline for you, are there?"

He was smiling but Suzy heard the hard edge to his voice and saw the way his fist was clenched round his glass of Scotch.

"Me? Good heavens no!" She laughed lightly, trying to ignore the thumping of her heart. "They keep me busy enough at the station already without . . ."

"Oh, well, aren't you the lucky one?" Edward's voice was sneering. "So popular, so busy, so much in demand. I'm going out."

"But, darling, it would be so nice to spend the evening together, to talk . . ."

"Oh yes!" Edward exploded. "So nice to talk! About you . . . always you, your success, your wonderful life . . ."

———

124

Furiously he swung his arm, spilling the contents of his glass all over Suzy's skirt.

Without pausing for a backward glance, he stormed through the hall and out of the front door.

Suzy stood, watching the stain seep slowly through the delicate material. Then with a quiet sob, she sank on to the sofa and buried her face in her hands.

———

"That pizza was to die for," said Sinead as they darted out of the restaurant and across the main road. "Hey, look out!"

She grabbed Nick's arm just as a fire engine streaked past, sirens wailing.

"Sorry," he said.

"Look," said Sinead, who had been waiting for the right moment but could wait no longer. "I don't know what's wrong, but at least your house isn't burning down, is it?"

Nick smiled. "I haven't been very good company, have I?" he said ruefully.

"No," said Sinead calmly. "But that's OK – I just wish I could help. I guess it has something to do with that man who was at your house?"

Nick said nothing.

"You can tell me to mind my own business," suggested Sinead.

"No," he murmured. "You're right – that guy – I'm pretty sure he's come to collect money my dad owed him.

It wasn't his fault – he just died at the wrong time – only Mum's been struggling to save up the deposit for a house – and she's nearly there and now he's come and . . . God, what a mess!"

"Well," replied Sinead resolutely, "if your mum does have to pay him, at least you can carry on staying at your gran's house. It's not as if you will be homeless."

Nick sighed. "That's easy for you to say," he muttered, "living in that swish apartment with oodles of space."

This time it was Sinead who looked downcast. "Sometimes I think we were better off when we lived at Burnthedge," she said. "At least Mum was happy then. Now that Dad's bought this racehorse . . ."

"Your dad owns a horse?" Nick looked gobsmacked. "I didn't know."

"There's a lot you don't know about me," murmured Sinead.

"I suppose there is," said Nick. "But I'm kind of looking forward to finding out."

And then, without meaning to for one moment, he stopped, put his hands on her shoulders and rather shyly kissed her briefly on the lips.

And then again. For rather longer.

And suddenly, Mike Lovell was the last thing on his mind.

———

That is so awful, thought Chloë, quietly closing the Flahertys' front door behind her. Now that Shaun and

Kathleen were home, she felt awkward witnessing their shock and distress and had crept away unnoticed.

She had reached the staircase when she heard footsteps.

"Dad!" One look at her father's face put her whole being on red alert. "Where are you going? What . . . ?"

"Hi, sunshine!" he said with a cheery smile. "Just dashing out for a bit – catch you later."

He ruffled her hair and sped on down the stairs.

Chloë stood still for an instant, and then galloped upstairs, two at a time. "Mum!" she called before her foot was inside the door. "Mum?"

"Darling!" Her mother jumped up from the sofa and came across to give her a hug.

"Mum, you're soaked!" Chloë wrinkled her nose at the familiar smell of Scotch.

"So silly," Suzy said. "Spilt my drink – just off to have a shower."

It occurred to Chloë, as she went into the kitchen for a cloth to mop up the damp patch on the carpet, that most grown women didn't have tears in their eyes over one spilled whisky.

Besides, her mother hated whisky. Her dad drank it every evening, but her mother never touched the stuff.

———

"Now drink this tea." Kathleen Flaherty put a steaming mug down on the coffee table, pausing to lay a hand on her husband's shaking shoulder.

"We'll sort this, Shaun love, you'll see," she said. "Erin, stop snivelling. Snivelling never helped anyone."

Erin sniffed and wiped her nose on the back of her hand.

Shaun rubbed a hand wearily over his forehead. "It's all gone, Kath," he said. "Just a pile of charred timbers and a whole lot of broken glass. All those wardrobes for Fred . . ."

"The ones he hadn't paid for," added Kathleen wryly.

Shaun nodded miserably. "And the new stock – got it this morning – for Declan's mate," he whispered. "I was going to start on the designs on Monday."

Kathleen paled and then pulled back her shoulders. "Well," she said stoically, "what can't be cured must be endured."

There was the sound of a key in the front door.

"That will be Sinead," said Kathleen. "No, you sit there – I'll tell her."

She crossed the sitting-room and was almost knocked over as Sinead burst into the room and flung her arms round her mother.

"Mum, I'm so happy I could burst! I want to tell the whole world, I . . . Dad?"

Her mother took her arm. "Sinead dear, there's something you should know. Your dad's workshop – there was a fire. Everything's been destroyed."

Sinead gasped and then ran over to her father. "Oh, Dad!" she cried, putting an arm round his shoulders. "At least you're safe – think how much worse it would have been if you'd been hurt."

"That's my girl," murmured Kathleen.

"Are we going to be poor again?" asked Erin.

Kathleen tutted in annoyance. "Of course not," she said impatiently. "We've got a bit of spending money left aside from the investments – and besides, there's the insurance. Your dad's not daft, you know."

There was a sharp intake of breath and Shaun bit down on his clenched fist. Then he slowly lifted his eyes and looked at his wife.

It was a look of abject misery.

"Shaun?" It was Kathleen's turn to go pale.

"The insurance," he croaked. "I forgot to renew the policy. It ran out last month. Oh, Kathleen, I . . ." His voice faltered.

No one spoke.

There seemed little any of them could say.

————

He'd kissed her! He had kissed Sinead. Her lips had been soft and warm and when she had run her fingers across the back of his neck, his whole body had tingled with little electric shocks.

He lifted his hands to his nose and smelt the faint woody aroma of her perfume. He wished he hadn't left it so late in the evening to kiss her – now she was gone and there was so much he wanted to say.

But he would see her on Monday. Not that he could

kiss her at school – Mr Lamport had a thing about what he called "consorting among the sexes" but there would be evenings and weekends and . . .

"Good evening!"

Nick looked up, startled out of his thoughts by a vaguely familiar voice. It was Mike Lovell.

Nick was about to speak, to demand to know why he was still hanging around his gran's house – but before he could say a word a taxi had pulled up at the kerb and Mike jumped in.

Mum! thought Nick, and ran full pelt down the road to his house. Mike must have been there for hours! If he had intimidated her – or worse still, made her hand over money she couldn't afford . . ."

"Nick! There you are – good evening?"

His mum was piling photo albums into the bookcase, looking remarkably cheerful for someone who had spent the last three hours with an angry creditor.

"Are you all right? What did that guy want? You didn't . . . ?"

His mum waved him towards an armchair. "Sit," she said.

He sat.

"Nick, Mike Lovell is an old university friend of your father's. He didn't know Dad was dead – and he's spent over a year trying to track us down."

Nick swallowed. "Why?"

"Because it seems that years ago, Dad helped Mike to

emigrate to Australia – lent him money, sponsored him through a college course – even kept an eye on his sister back here in England."

Nick looked amazed. "Dad never said anything about this," he said suspiciously. "Are you sure this Mike guy isn't some sort of con artist?"

"Oh, for heaven's sake!" exclaimed his mother. "Look!"

She grabbed one of the photo albums. "There's Dad at his graduation – and there's Mike. See? In the row behind?"

Nick peered at the somewhat faded photograph. It was unmistakably the same guy who had arrived on their doorstep.

"He came hoping to find Dad," continued Jenny. "He'd had his Christmas card returned from Italy marked 'Gone Away'."

"So," queried Nick, "how did he find us?"

"Ever so clever – just like that detective thing on the telly!" His gran bustled into the room in her dressing-gown and a fetching set of bright pink rollers. "Tell him, Jenny!"

Nick's mum grinned. "Dad had told him in a letter that you were at boarding school in Sussex," said Jenny. "Do you know, he phoned every boys' school until he found the right one? Of course, the headmaster wouldn't give out your address but he did say that we'd moved to the Leeds area."

Even Nick was impressed. "You mean he wanted to see Dad that much?"

Jenny nodded, her eyes misting slightly. "He said that Greg was the best mate . . ."

"Buddy, that's what he said," corrected Nick's gran. "Buddy."

"OK, buddy," conceded Jenny. "The best buddy he had ever had – solid, dependable, funny . . ."

Nick nodded. "I wish," he said after a pause, "that I hadn't been so – well, you know . . ."

"Rude?" queried his mother.

Nick nodded ruefully.

"Don't worry," she said. "You'll have a chance to apologise. He's over here for a few more weeks. And very soon, he's coming to dinner."

"Great!" exclaimed Nick. And actually meant it.

Chapter 12

A FEW BREAKDOWNS IN COMMUNICATION

"Sinead?"

Chloë tapped her friend's shoulder as they filed into registration on Monday morning.

Sinead looked round.

"Look, I'm really sorry about what happened to your dad's workshop," Chloë said. "Is he OK?"

"Pretty cut up," Sinead replied. "See, he forgot to renew the insurance, so . . ."

Chloë gasped. "You mean – you won't get any money back."

"Precisely," said Sinead.

Chloë shook her head in disbelief. "Your mum must be in pieces," she gasped.

Sinead frowned. "You know, it's odd," she said. "But this weekend she's been more bouncy and more like her old self than she has for months. I was saying to Nick yesterday . . ."

"You were with Nick yesterday as well as Saturday?" Chloë's expression of caring compassion disappeared to be replaced with a look of pure venom.

Sinead nodded. "We went for this lovely long walk all round Eccup reservoir, and then we had ice cream . . ."

"Spare me the details!" snapped Chloë. "Look – I think you and I should have a chat."

"Really?" Sinead looked at her, wide-eyed. "What about?"

"Meet me at break," ordered Chloë. "I'll tell you then."

In words of one syllable, she added silently in her head.

———

"Well, I have to admit, it's all pretty impressive!" Sanjay's father stood, hands behind his back, surveying the Computer Graphics lab at Beckendon College. "What do you say, Sanjay?"

"It's . . . it's . . ." Sanjay struggled to find words to express the jumble of impressions in his brain. It was great, of course it was, this part of it. But the rest . . . no way could he do it. No way could he come here.

"It's amazing," he said, as they walked over to the corridor where they had been instructed to wait. Amazing, but not for him.

It wasn't just the size of the place; he guessed he would get used to that in time. But each landing in the residential block had a shared kitchen and a block of communal showers. There had been guys in one of the kitchens, cooking up a paella for someone's birthday; in the bathroom someone was doing a pile of washing to the deafening sound of reggae blaring from an old radio. And everyone looked so much more grown-up than him.

"Sanjay Fraser!" A large oak door opened and a secretary beckoned to him. "The selection board are ready for you now."

"Good luck, darling!" whispered his mum.

"Show them what you're made of!" encouraged his father, who appeared to have undertaken a total change of heart.

Sanjay gulped. His mouth began to go dry, his heart quickened and the palms of his hands grew moist. He was quite sure that his legs would give way under him before he managed to cross the vast, cream-carpeted room to the black leather chair facing the five interviewers.

He fingered the Good Luck card buried in his jacket pocket. Jasmin had written *Win or lose, I'll love you for ever.*

Well, at least he wouldn't have to leave her. At least they could carry on as normal.

Always assuming he didn't die of heart failure within the next ten minutes.

———

"Josie, I have to have your answer. I can't wait for ever."

Alex looked Josephine directly in the eyes.

"You know you want to do it," he said. "What's stopping you?"

Josie turned away impatiently. "What's stopping me?" she repeated. "I have responsibilities – to my husband, my daughter – and the business to help run . . ."

"A business you don't enjoy," reasoned Alex. "Is it unreasonable to want a bit of happiness for yourself?"

Josie said nothing.

"Look," said Alex, "I have to go away tomorrow for two weeks. On a business trip."

"By the time I get back I want an answer. Yes or no. I mean it, Josie."

Slowly Josie nodded. "OK," she said softly. "Two weeks. I'll tell you then. I promise."

He squeezed her hand. "Great," he said. "Now, do I get a hug before I go?"

———

"So you see," said Chloë, pulling up a chair next to Sinead at the back of the library, "I don't want you to be hurt. Nick's only hanging round you because I gave him the cold shoulder. He's using you, Sinead."

She paused for dramatic effect. "And I can't bear that to happen to a friend of mine," she concluded.

Sinead said nothing, but nibbled at a fingernail.

"Don't you remember," Chloë pressed on, "that you kept telling me all last term that Nick fancied me?"

Sinead nodded.

"You were right, of course," added Chloë, gaining

confidence. "Only I was so caught up with that jerk Jack that I didn't realise."

Always admit your part in the situation – that's what that How To Get What You Want Right Now article had said.

Still Sinead said nothing.

"So I reckon you should steer clear," advised Chloë. "Because, as soon as he realises that it's me he really wants, he'll drop you without a second thought."

Sinead nodded thoughtfully.

"I'm so glad you agree," said Chloë, relief swamping her as she gave Sinead a hug.

"But I don't," smiled Sinead.

"What?"

"I don't agree."

"Haven't you listened to a word I've been saying?" demanded Chloë.

"Oh yes," said Sinead. "I've listened. But I think I'll just take my chances. If he drops me, he drops me."

Chloë was speechless.

"But in the meantime," said Sinead, with a wicked grin on her face, "I'm having the best time ever. Must dash!" And with that she jumped up, grabbed her bag and pushed through the swing doors and into the corridor.

Right! thought Chloë. You want to play it that way? I'll show you. Just you wait, Sinead Flaherty. Just you wait.

———

"Well, I hear you put the cat amongst the pigeons last week, Suzy Sanderson!"

Suzy looked up from her desk to Hannah Brooks, the station's resident agony aunt, grinning down at her.

"Refusing to interview the great Isla Idris? Most of us would die for the opportunity."

"Oh really?" retorted Suzy, rather more irritably than she had intended.

"Seriously, Suzy love, Nathan's not amused. In fact, between you and me, he's putting in an official complaint to the powers that be. People have been sacked for less, you know."

Suzy caught her breath and looked at Hannah.

"I'd apologise and say you'll do it, if I were you," encouraged the agony aunt kindly.

Suzy leaped to her feet. "Well, you're not me, are you, Hannah? So perhaps instead of coming on strong with the good advice, you'd just leave me alone to get on with writing my script and . . ."

"OK, OK, keep your hair on!" Hannah took a step back. "It's just not like you, that's all – and you have to admit, this new film of Isla's is going to make headlines. They say it's the most realistic portrayal of domestic violence in all its horror that has ever . . ."

"Oh do they?" Suzy's voice cracked, and she jumped up, pushing Hannah out of the way and running to the door of the production office. "Well, if you're so interested in it, why don't you do the damn interview yourself?"

She wrenched open the door.

"Aaah!" Suzy managed to suppress the yelp of pain from her bruised wrist but not before Hannah had noticed.

"Oh my God!" Hannah breathed as Suzy slammed the door. "Don't tell me – I mean, that can't surely be why she won't interview Isla. Please, please – not that."

She picked up her bag, crossed to the door and stopped. Now was not the right time to say anything.

But there would be a good time.

And Hannah knew she would have to say something. Because unless she was very much mistaken, Suzy was in danger of losing something far more important than her job.

———

"Harry?" Josephine tapped her husband on the shoulder. "Want any help with the boat?"

Harry looked up from his sanding of the deck, his expression one of total astonishment. "Well, yes, love, that would be great," he beamed. "If you really don't mind."

For a few minutes they worked in companionable silence, and then Josie flopped down on the deck. "Harry?" she said again.

"Mmmm?"

"Have you ever thought of selling out to one of the big chains?" she said in a rush.

"Selling?" Her husband looked at her, astonished.

Josie nodded. "To someone like Café Rouge or . . ."

"No I have not!" exploded Harry. "This place is a little gold mine and besides, I've got such plans – you wait till this boat is done and we've got . . ."

"I'm not asking you to leave," insisted Josie. "I just thought if someone bought a share – well . . ."

"Well what?"

Josie bit her lip. I could do something different, she thought. I could follow my dream. I could . . .

"Nothing," she said with a weak grin. "Forget it. Now, what I am supposed to do with this chisel?"

———

Jenny Bowen wandered back into the café deep in thought. She hadn't meant to eavesdrop but she had been bringing Harry his lunch-time sandwich and couldn't help overhearing.

If Josie did persuade Harry to sell a share in the restaurant, she would lose her job. Big restaurant chains didn't employ managers with no qualifications, and certainly didn't give them the freedom she got here. Only last week she had done half the cooking when Anton burned his hand, and Harry had promised that she could run a clam bake in the summer.

She couldn't think why Josie was so dissatisfied. She certainly didn't love the café like Jenny did. She never seemed to get caught up in the excitement of new menus, new ideas, new customers.

And clearly she didn't get a buzz from feeling it was all hers.

Otherwise she couldn't contemplate selling even a tenth of it to somebody else.

———

Sinead sat in the loo and wiped her eyes on a piece of toilet paper. Was Chloë right? Was Nick just using her to make Chloë jealous? If so, it was working – she was quite definitely spitting bullets.

I love him, Sinead whispered to herself. I can't help it. I won't stop loving him even if he walks away from me tomorrow.

She closed her eyes, remembering that long, lingering kiss, the amazing sensations of warmth that had coursed through her body, the way his fingers had delicately traced the outline of her nose and mouth.

She shuddered.

She loved him. She wanted him. She needed him.

She could face all the troubles at home, the pressures of exams – everything, as long as she had Nick.

He was the best thing that had ever happened to her.

And she wasn't going to give him up without a fight.

———

"So, how did it go, son?"

Sanjay's father leaped up enthusiastically as Sanjay emerged from the interview room.

"OK," said Sanjay diffidently. "It was hard."

"Hard? What do you mean, hard? You're a bright enough lad – you didn't go and blow it, did you?"

It was remarkable, thought Sanjay wryly, that his

father, who for months had mocked him for wanting to become an animation expert, was now totally sold on the idea of this course.

"So what did they ask you? You did mention me, didn't you? Academic parents carry weight, you know."

"We talked about Mum's new novel," Sanjay ventured.

"You did WHAT? Oh well, that's it, then. If all you can talk about is some foolish, romantic . . ."

"They were asking questions about cross-media imagery," Sanjay began. "It's fascinating, Dad. Did you know . . . ?"

Sanjay launched into a detailed account of procedures about which his father clearly knew nothing. He knew he was boring his dad rigid, but he kept talking. It was quite nice to be the one with the power for a change.

———

"So will you?" Jasmin nudged Sinead over lunch.

"Will I what?"

Sinead had clearly been thinking of other things.

"Help paint the boat," repeated Jasmin. "Dad's dead keen to get it done in time for the May bank holiday."

"Well . . ."

"I mean, we can't spend the whole Easter holidays revising, can we? Our brains would seize up."

Sinead grinned. "I'll ask Nick," she said. "If he's up for it, so am I. Only . . ."

"Only what?"

"Chloë didn't put you up to this, did she?"

Jasmin frowned. "No? Why should she?"

"No reason," said Sinead.

———

"If you want to, we can, I guess."

Nick did not sound too enthusiastic.

"Not if you don't like the idea," said Sinead hastily.

"Well . . ." Nick hesitated. "Actually, I'd like to spend a lot of time with you – on our own. If you don't mind . . ."

Sinead couldn't suppress the broad grin that spread over her face. "Really?" she said. "Do you mean that?"

Nick put his arm round her and gave her a squeeze. "Of course I do, silly," he said. "Who else would I want to be with?"

This, thought Sinead, leaning her head against his shoulder, is what they mean by perfect happiness.

———

Kathleen walked out of the bank, blinking as the bright sunlight hit her eyes. Four hundred and thirty-eight thousand, five hundred pounds. He had spent almost half a million. No, she told herself firmly, let's be fair. *We* have spent almost half a million.

Of course, the flat had cost over two hundred thousand pounds. And then there had been the holidays, and the new car, and all the furniture. But where had the rest gone?

The horse, of course. The stock for Shaun's business.

But still.

Kathleen felt slightly sick.

All that was left was about twenty thousand pounds in cash and the money they'd invested for the future.

And no way were they going to touch that. From now on, they were going to have to be seriously sensible.

Shaun would hate it. The girls wouldn't think much of it, either.

But funnily enough, it didn't bother her. This, she thought, was a lot more like reality than anything she had lived through in the last twelve months.

Chapter 13

CHANGES AFOOT

"HI, CHLOË, it's Jasmin. Are you OK?"

"Yes, fine. Why?" Chloë gripped the receiver and tried to sound bright and cheerful.

"Cold better?"

"What cold . . . oh, that. Yes, false alarm, I guess."

"Great," said Jasmin. "So – what time tomorrow?"

"Tomorrow?"

"MegaSport UK – what time shall we meet?"

Chloë thought fast. She had forgotten all about this dumb sports festival and, suddenly, the last thing on earth she wanted to do was go out for the day, pretending that everything was terrific. Besides, her mum might still be off work tomorrow and no way was Chloë going anywhere if she was. Not with her dad prowling around the house not speaking.

"Look, I can't make it after all," she said rapidly. "You go."

"I'm not going without you," protested Jasmin. "Remember, I only agreed because you begged me. And remember, if you don't go, Sinead and Nick will be on their own," she added teasingly.

"Stuff Nick and Sinead!" shouted Chloë. "I really don't care, OK?"

"OK," said Jasmin. "See you at school the day after tomorrow, yeah?"

She put down the phone and stared thoughtfully out of the window. Something was wrong. Chloë was behaving very oddly – not just her pretending not to mind about Sinead and Nick.

It had to be because there was something far more important on Chloë's mind. And from what Jasmin could tell, it wasn't something that was giving her any joy at all.

———

Two hours later, Chloë was flicking idly through her History notes, hardly seeing what was written on the page. She couldn't believe that her mum had insisted on going into the office. Although there were no visible bruises to attract attention, anyone could see from the way she walked that she was in agony – and judging from the black lines under her eyes, she hadn't slept much either. The TV station had found someone to cover the breakfast show, so why couldn't her mum have taken the day off? It didn't make sense.

I guess I could have gone to the sports festival, she

thought. With Mum back at work there's no need to be here. But somehow it was all too much effort – dressing up, coming on to Nick, when clearly he was far more interested in Sinead. Besides, what was the point? If you got close to someone, they started asking questions, wanting to meet your family, come round to your house. And that meant more pretending. Right now, Chloë felt as if she had done enough pretending to last her a lifetime.

She tried to concentrate on the causes of the Vietnam War, but the words kept blurring before her eyes. It wasn't until the ink began to smudge that she realised she was crying.

And that she couldn't stop.

———

"Suzy! They said you weren't well!" Hannah Brooks stood up as Suzy walked through the main office, her eyes narrowing as they came to rest on her friend's careworn face.

She moved towards her, opened her arms and gave her a hug.

"AAAH!! No, don't!" Suzy's face blanched as she pulled away, clasping her hands to her ribs.

"Suzy? What is it? What's wrong?"

Smile, Suzy ordered herself firmly. Shoulders back, head up. Smile.

"Oh, Hannah, Hannah!" she sobbed, her shoulders heaving. "What am I going to do?"

———

"Oh, Suzy!" Hannah's face was contorted with pain as Chloë's mum finally paused for breath. "Well, one thing is certain; you have to leave him."

"But I can't!" Suzy replied instantly. "It's impossible."

"Why?" demanded Hannah. "You're financially independent, you've got a good job . . ."

"That's precisely it," interrupted Suzy. "I'm famous."

"So? Because you're famous, that means you have to put up with being beaten, does it? Suzy, get real. Surely you must have thought about going?"

Suzy nodded, rubbing her sore neck. "Yes, of course I have. Only the time is never right – when Chloë was a baby, I said I'd wait till she was at school; then I put it off till she was at secondary school, but then . . ."

"Hang on!" interjected Hannah. "Are you telling me that this – this thug has been beating you since Chloë was tiny?"

Suzy bit her lip. "Since the second week of our honeymoon," she whispered. "He doesn't mean it, though – you have to understand that . . ."

"SUZY!" Hannah's voice was stern. "Listen to me. There is one thing, and one thing only, that I understand about this ghastly situation and that is that you have to do something. Not just for you, but for Chloë too. What do you think it's like for her, living under the threat of violence all the time?"

"Oh, but her father would never lay a finger on her," protested Suzy.

"And you think that makes it all right? The poor kid must be terrified for your safety. Look, Suzy, the time for hoping and enduring and burying your head in the sand is over."

"But . . ."

Hannah took Suzy's hands in her own. "Get out, Suzy, get out of that marriage. Now. Before it's too late."

For a long moment, Suzy stared silently at Hannah. And then slowly, very slowly, she began to nod her head.

———

"I can't see any other way out. We're going to have to move." Kathleen Flaherty sat calmly at the dining-room table, surveying her family's assorted expressions.

"Leave The Wharfside?" Shaun gasped.

"Move? Again?" stammered Sinead.

"We are not going back to Burnthedge, are we?" pleaded Erin.

Kathleen shook her head. "Of course not," she said, smiling reassuringly. "There are some very nice four-bedroomed houses about for around one hundred and fifty thousand pounds – and that would leave us a good seventy-five thousand clear after selling this place."

She moved her pile of papers. "And then once the horse has been sold . . ."

"No!" This time Shaun's voice was stronger. "Please – not yet. I mean, there's these races coming up and I just know Toffee Apple's going to give a good showing of himself. We could win thousands in prize money."

Kathleen chewed her lip. She knew full well he was living in cloud cuckoo land, but he'd been to hell and back over the past week or so, waking up at night, racked with guilt, and just picking at his food. Poor lamb, he deserved something to hang on to.

"All right," she conceded. "We'll keep the confounded horse until June – but if it's not paying its way, it goes. Agreed?"

"Agreed," sighed Shaun with relief.

"And that Declan can start putting his money where his mouth is and all," muttered Kathleen. "Now listen."

She turned to the girls.

"We're in this together, right? We are still a lot better off than we ever were in the old days, and when we move we will still be living in a far nicer house than that heap at Burnthedge. So I don't want any long faces or moans and groans, is that understood? The Lord giveth and the Lord taketh way, that's what Father Ryan says."

"I thought," said Shaun with a rare grin, "that you thought Father Ryan talked a lot of rubbish."

Kathleen sniffed. "He has his moments," she said. "Now if you don't mind, I'm on dinner duty at the school."

"What about our dinner?" protested Erin.

"You know where the fridge is," said her mother. And went. Without even noticing the crumpled newspapers on the sofa or the half empty cup of coffee standing on the sideboard.

———

"Mike! That's impossible – I mean, you can't – we can't – it's crazy!"

Jenny Bowen stared at Mike in disbelief at his suggestion.

"Not crazy at all," he said calmly. "I have the money, you have the know-how, and from what you tell me there's a whole load of potential for a brilliant business. At least let me find out what they say."

"But you can't – I mean, they won't – and anyway, I don't accept favours."

"It's not a favour," he replied sternly. "Strictly business: I put the money up front, I take a profit share, you pay back the loan at two per cent interest . . ."

"That's ridiculously low . . ."

"Oh be quiet!" Mike laughed. "Just let me make the enquiries, OK?"

Slowly Jenny nodded. "OK," she said. "But strictly business, you understand."

"I never doubted it for a moment," smiled Mike.

Chapter 14

CONFESSION TIME

"AND NOW, some splendid news to start the new term!" The headmaster beamed beatifically at the assembled group of Year Ten and Eleven students and clasped his hands behind his back.

"Sanjay Fraser has been awarded the Louis Breançon Scholarship to Beckendon College – an achievement indeed!"

After the clapping had died down, Nick leaned across to his friend. "You dark horse!" he whispered. "Why didn't you tell me?"

Because I don't want to go, because I wish I had never taken the interview, because I'm scared to death even thinking about it, replied Sanjay in the silence of his head.

"I forgot," he whispered back. "Anyway, I might not go."

"You WHAT?" gasped Nick. "Don't tell me – your dad's playing up again, right?"

Sanjay was about to agree. After all, everyone knew what a stuffed shirt his dad was – or rather, had been. No one would be surprised. He could just blame him and stay on at Lockbridge and everything would carry on as usual.

But even as the thought ran through his mind, he knew he couldn't. For one thing, it wasn't his dad – Duncan seized every opportunity to tell his friends that his son was the Breançon Scholar. And for another, things never stayed the same. For better or worse, things changed. Even if he didn't go to London now, in another couple of years he'd be off to university. He had to grow up some time.

And he wanted to make Jasmin proud of him. One day he was going to marry her. He hadn't asked her yet, of course, but . . . well, after the exams were over, he would.

Then maybe he'd feel better about leaving. Once he knew that she was well and truly his.

––––––

"I can't believe they've come!" wailed Sinead on the morning of the first GCSE exam. "I can't remember a thing – I just know I'm going to fail the lot!"

"Oh puh-leese!" sighed Jasmin. "As if! Besides, you've got lots of ferry-whatsits . . ."

"Pardon?"

"Those things you get buzzing through your brain when you're in love," grinned Jasmin. "They make you fire on all cylinders."

"Well," sighed Sinead, "I wish they'd start. See you after Physics. Oh heck."

———

While Jasmin was giving her friend a pep talk, her mother was receiving an unexpected visitor in the café.

"Mrs Johnson, I'm Mike Lovell – you may remember I've been here for quite a few meals lately."

"Oh yes," said Josie, dumping a pile of menus on the table and offering her hand. "Jenny's friend. I'm afraid you're out of luck – it's her day off today."

"That's why I'm here!" said Mike cheerfully. "You see, I have a proposition to put to you."

Josie frowned. "To me? What do you mean?" She gestured towards a chair.

"Two coffees and some cakes, please, Anton!" she called. "Now, Mr Lovell . . ."

"Mike, please."

"Mike. What can I do for you?"

Mike clasped his hands together and leaned towards her enthusiastically. "I am rather hoping," he said, "that you will sell me – well, Jenny really – a share in this rather splendid eatery."

———

I do hope, thought Nick two days later as he gave up on even trying to do any more of his German paper, that Mum isn't falling in love with Mike. They seem to be spending an awful lot of time together for people who only met a month ago.

I mean, he's a nice enough guy and all that – but I don't want anyone trying to take the place of Dad. And besides, he lives in Australia, and I'm perfectly happy here in Leeds, thank you.

He laughed quietly to himself. If someone had told him six months before that he would be thinking like that, he would have told them they were crazy. But now, with things going so well with Sinead, and his mum starting to bring estate agents' details home every night, life was really looking up.

Or would be if he could fathom out what this stupid translation meant. Mind you, German wasn't essential for someone who had just decided to do Sports Sciences at university. So if he failed, he failed.

He put the top on his pen, leaned back in his chair and began reliving that rather special kiss Sinead had given him the night before.

———

Jasmin planted the final full stop at the end of her English Literature paper, stretched and tried to shake some life back into her aching wrist. Only two more exams to go, thank goodness.

She glanced across the examination room to where Chloë was sitting. She wasn't writing a word. She was gazing out of the window, rubbing her hands together, pulling at strands of hair, biting her fingernails. Jasmin sighed. She wished there was something she could do. She felt so useless, knowing that Chloë was in some sort of trouble and yet not being able to reach her.

"Time's up – stop writing, boys and girls!" demanded the invigilator. There was the noise of chairs being scraped, sighs being expelled, pens being dropped. And then suddenly, Chloë stood up and sped from the room, slamming the door behind her.

The moment her paper was collected, Jasmin grabbed her bag and hurried after her. The time for being polite and tactful was over. She was going to find out what was wrong once and for all.

———

Jasmin had tried all the obvious places – the loos, the locker room, the library. To no avail. There was no sign of Chloë.

There was nothing for it but to go back to her classroom and get ready for her Art exam. Chloë didn't do Art. She must have gone home.

Jasmin was about to take the forbidden short cut up the fire escape steps when she saw her. She was sitting on the bench at the back of the Music block, her head in her hands.

And she was crying.

"Chloë!" Jasmin was at her side in seconds. "What is it? Please tell me what's wrong."

She waited for all the usual denials, the feeble excuses, or the orders to get lost. They didn't come.

Chloë raised a tear-stained face and stared at her. "I can't cope any more, Jasmin," she sobbed. "I don't know what to do and I'm so scared!"

And with that she threw herself into Jasmin's arms and wept as though her heart would break.

———

"And you promise, faithfully, that you won't tell a living soul?" Chloë pleaded for the third time.

"If that's what you want," agreed Jasmin. "Listen, I just want to say this, and then I'll never mention it again, OK?"

Chloë nodded.

"No one ever should have to go through what your mum has gone through," she said firmly. "My dad got beaten up in the street by a pair of thugs and that was bad enough. It's taken him two years to get over it. But your mum is being hurt on a regular basis by someone who is supposed to love her. That's a million times worse."

"I know," whispered Chloë. "I hate him."

Jasmin nodded thoughtfully. "But you love him too, right?" she said. "And that makes it all even harder."

Chloë stared at her. "So you understand," she breathed.

Jasmin nodded. "I think so," she said. "I don't know what you should do but I just want you to know that I'm here if you need me. And I won't breathe a word to a soul – but shouldn't you see Mrs Braithwaite? Or the school nurse? Or someone?"

Chloë shook her head. "I feel better now I've got you to talk to," she said. "I can talk to you, can't I? I mean, if . . ." Her voice trailed off.

"You can talk to me whenever you like," said Jasmin, squeezing her hand. "We're friends, remember?"

———

If May passed in a blur of exams for the gang of five, it wasn't exactly uneventful for their parents. While Sinead's mum had a very successful month house-hunting and locating at least three houses which she thought would do them very nicely, Toffee Apple had a singularly disastrous début into the world of racing.

At Doncaster, he forgot to leave the starting stalls and never managed to catch up with the rest of the field; at York he galloped away quite merrily for two furlongs and then lost all interest, shied at a fence post, threw his jockey on the ground and was munching grass while the rest of the field passed the winning post.

"Don't worry," Shaun reassured his family before Toffee Apple's third – and according to Kathleen, last – attempt to make a name for himself. "We've decided he needs a longer distance, more time to get his pace going."

"What pace?" giggled Sinead.

"You'll be laughing on the other side of your face in a fortnight," warned Shaun. "Redcar, three fifteen. That's when you'll see what he's made of."

"If you don't mind," muttered Kathleen, "I'll not be holding my breath."

———

"Suzy – I don't know what to say," repeated Nathan for the third time that morning. "I mean – resigning? Isn't that a bit drastic? Just because you got a reprimand over one interview?"

Suzy smiled and glanced round the TV producer's cluttered office. "It has nothing to do with that," she said. "I've got a job in London – at the BBC. They needed someone to host a lunch-time programme and they approached me. I'm sorry to leave, Nathan, but it's an amazing opportunity and it's what I need – a new start."

"And what does Edward think about all this?" Nathan asked.

"He doesn't know," said Suzy. "Nathan, I think there is something I should tell you. But if I ever hear that you have spoken to another living soul about this, I shall never speak to you again. Is that quite clear?"

Nathan nodded.

"Very well," said Suzy. "The thing is . . ."

———

While Suzy was speaking the unspeakable at the headquarters of Pennine TV, Jasmin's mum was plying her husband with red wine and praying that he would be reasonable.

"And you know that Jenny is far more enthusiastic about this place than I am," she said. "She'd make you a far better business partner – she has amazing ideas, and this investment would mean you could finish the boat and build that balcony and . . ."

"Great!" said Harry. "Absolutely terrific!"

"You mean," gasped Josephine, "you don't mind?

About my pulling out? Taking my share of cash out of the business?"

Harry gave her a hug. "Darling, I've known for ages that this isn't your scene. I mean, the only days you are really bouncy and full of life is when you've been singing in your choir or off on a concert trip. I may be scarred but I'm not blind."

Josie squeezed his hand. "Has it been so obvious?" she said.

"Yup," replied Harry. "So what are you going to do with all this money you'll be pulling out of the business?"

"Ah," said Josie. "Now that's the other thing I wanted to talk to you about . . ."

———

Chloë stood in front of the locker-room mirror, dabbing her eyes and praying that no one would see that she had been crying. It seemed like she spent half her life in tears these days. OK, so the Biology paper was the pits and the History more dire than she would have believed, but it was useless crying about it.

And what if Dad did keep begging her to be more friendly, calling her his princess and telling her that from now on life was going to be different? She wanted to believe him but she was sixteen and a half and not dumb. Nothing would be different. But she couldn't help wishing it was.

"Chloë." In the mirror, Chloë saw Sinead come up behind her. "Look, I know why you're so upset these days. Jasmin told me."

"She did WHAT?" I don't believe it, thought Chloë. Not Jasmin. She swore she wouldn't say a word.

"I know you're upset about me and Nick," continued Sinead. "And honestly, I am sorry. Not about him and me being together – but about the fact that I did try really hard to get him off you. And that was mean."

Chloë was so relieved that she gave Sinead a spontaneous hug. "Silly," she said. "Nick's the least of my wo . . . I mean, I don't want Nick."

"You don't?"

"No." It wasn't quite true, but at least this way she would keep a bit of dignity. "I guess what I wanted was a guy. Any guy. And Nick seemed available."

Sinead still looked worried.

"Look," said Chloë. "Don't worry. I'm not about to start trying to wheedle my way into his affections. It would be pointless. It's you he loves."

"Do you really think so?"

"I know so," said Chloë. "I just hope one day I find a guy who really loves me."

Only they say they do and then they hit you and . . . She could feel the tears welling up again. Stop it.

"You will," Sinead assured her. "Are we still friends?"

"Of course," said Chloë. "I am expecting to be bridesmaid."

Sinead burst out laughing and for the first time in a long while, Chloë found herself giggling too.

She slipped her arm through Sinead's and suggested a quick detour to the tuck shop.

———

It was on the day of the very last GCSE exam that Jasmin got her shock. If she hadn't forgotten her lucky four-leaf clover and sped back along the canalside and into the café to collect it, she would never have overheard the conversation. But as she reached the foot of the stairs up to the flat, she heard voices coming from the tiny office.

She paused, straining to hear what was being said behind the half-open door.

"So you told him?" It was that man – that Alex Grainger. Jasmin stepped silently backwards and pressed herself up against the wall. "Was he very upset?"

Jasmin's mouth went dry.

"Actually," she heard her mother say, "he was remarkably nice about it. I told him about you – about what we planned – and he said that if that was really what I wanted, and if I was sure it would make me happy, we had his blessing."

"Darling, that's wonderful! I can't tell you how happy this makes me – I just knew the moment I met you that you were the one . . ."

Jasmin gasped and tears sprung into her eyes. Despite everything she'd said she hadn't believed it was true. She couldn't believe that her mum really was having an affair . . .

". . . I just know that the SongBus is going to make

such a difference to the lives of so many children in Leeds. It just needed the right person to organise it. Someone with a passion for music, and who could inspire all those disadvantaged kids – show them something different to a life of drugs and crime. You can work with them – set up choirs, gospel groups, pop groups . . ." Alex's excited voice tailed off.

Jasmin slumped against the wall, her heart racing. Song bus? Disadvantaged kids? Her cheeks felt hot with embarrassment and relief. If her mum knew what she had thought . . . Quietly she turned and crept down the stairs. She didn't need a lucky charm. Today, she felt that everything would go OK.

Chapter 16

SO THAT'S THAT, THEN!

"I CAN'T believe it, Nick!" cried Jenny, enveloping him in a hug. "I'm a company director – well, a café director, anyway!"

"And we really can move?" asked Nick. "You can afford it?"

"Just," nodded Jenny. "Nothing grand, mind you. Actually I saw one of those new two-bedroomed houses up on Clifton Crescent today and . . ."

"Clifton Crescent?" said Nick. "Great – take it, Mum."

Jenny frowned. "But you haven't even seen it yet," she protested.

"It'll be fine," Nick assured her. "Just do it, before it goes."

He didn't mention that Clifton Crescent backed on to the Cottage Gardens development where Sinead's family were moving the following month.

He thought that for now he'd keep quiet about it. Parents tended to go so over the top about relationships.

———

"It's Capri Boy and Trojan Début neck and neck," cried the commentator at Redcar racecourse. "They're followed by Fiddler's Fortune, then Eshrah, then, some way behind, it's Toffee Apple . . ."

"Toffee Apple! Toffee Apple!" shrieked Erin, grabbing Sinead's arm. "He mentioned Toffee Apple."

"He's lying fifth!" exclaimed Shaun.

"Shaun," said Kathleen, "there are only six horses in the race."

"And Toffee Apple's been pulled up – seems to be limping."

"Oh no!" gasped Shaun. "That's that, then."

"I rather think," said Kathleen, "that it is."

———

"Mum! What's going on?" Chloë arrived home four days before the end of term to find the hallway blocked with three huge suitcases and a couple of dress carriers.

Suzy came up to her and took her hands. "Chloë, darling," she said. "I wanted to wait until the end of term but I can't. We're leaving, Chloë. Now."

Chloë's eyes widened as she struggled to grasp what her mother was saying.

"Leaving?"

Suzy nodded slowly. "Today, after you'd left for school, Dad was in a terrible mood. I won't go into the whole thing, but suffice to say, he raised his hand and picked up a vase and . . . I knew. I'd had enough."

Chloë swallowed hard.

"Darling, this is hard for you," said her mother. "Believe me, I know that. But – would you be desperately, horribly upset if we moved? I mean, really moved – away from Leeds?"

Chloë gasped. "Away? Where to? What about school? I . . ."

Suzy led her into the sitting-room and gestured to her to sit down. "I've been offered a wonderful new job – a promotion, really . . ."

"Mum, that's brilliant!" cried Chloë and then frowned. "But what about the breakfast show?"

"Finished, done, over," smiled her mother. "I couldn't commute from London and . . ."

"London?" Chloë looked aghast.

"Perhaps I'd better start at the beginning," said her mother.

"Perhaps," said Chloë, "you had."

———

Sanjay and Jasmin walked hand-in-hand beside the canal. No more exams! And soon, no more school! A whole summer to spend being together and then . . .

"I can't bear to think of how much I'll miss you." Sanjay stopped walking and looked into Jasmin's eyes earnestly.

"Me too." She smiled sadly. "But we've got the whole summer – let's not think about it now – and afterwards,

———

we'll have the whole of the rest of our lives . . ."

"Yes. For ever. It'll be so wonderful," he said, bending to kiss her gently. Then smiled. "But who's going to tell your mother – you or me . . . ?"

––––––

"And what about Dad?" Chloë asked her mum as they sat over tea and shortbread.

"We are getting a divorce," said Suzy. "He says he'll contest it, he says he'll fight to keep me . . ."

"Fighting is all he knows," muttered Chloë.

"You must remember that he loves you," said her mum. "You can see him whenever you want, spend holidays with him . . ."

"No thanks," said Chloë. "Remember – I've lived with what he's done to you all my life. Oh, I'll see him for the odd day occasionally, I guess. But I can't love or respect anyone who does what he did. No way."

Suzy squeezed her hand. "So you'll decide what you want to do? Stay at Lockbridge High and live with Dad in the term-time or come to London with me and do your A levels at college."

Chloë took a deep breath. "I guess it's not up to me," she said.

"Of course it is, darling," cried her mum. "I'd never make you do anything you felt uncomfortable with."

"I know," nodded Chloë. "It's not that – it's the exams. Mum, I think I've blown them. I've been so uptight and . . ."

She choked back tears. "I guess I won't get a chance to do A levels."

Her mum stepped closer and wrapped her in a big hug. "I'm sure you're wrong, darling," she murmured. "But either way, I guess what we both need is a fresh start. So you're coming with me?"

"Of course," said Chloë with a watery grin. "However, there is one thing . . ."

"What's that, darling?"

"This hotel we are staying in till term ends," said Chloë. "Does it have a function room?"

"Yes," said Suzy.

"Oh good," said Chloë. "Can I have a mega-huge party before we go?"

———

"You're moving to London? Really?" Jasmin cried. "That's so brilliant."

"Oh well, thanks," said Chloë. "What about the 'I'll miss you so much, Chloë' bit?"

Jasmin pulled a face. "Of course I'll miss you, but don't you see? It's divine intervention."

"It is?"

Jasmin nodded. "I can come and stay with you, which my mum will approve of because she thinks you are a good influence, although heaven knows why . . ."

". . . and you can spend the whole time seeing Sanjay, is that it?" finished Chloë.

Jasmin nodded. "And then you can come back up here,

and stay with me, and by then Sinead will have gone off Nick and you can have him . . ."

"I don't want him," smiled Chloë. "I don't think I ever wanted *him*, just a guy to hang out with, someone to make me feel I mattered."

"But you do matter, guy or no guy," protested Jasmin.

"Yes. I think I'm starting to realise that now," said Chloë. "Now, are you going to help me plan this party or not?"

———

None of them had dared to think about this moment. All through the party they had danced and sung and drunk punch and talked about anything and everything except what was on all their minds.

It was Nick who put it into words.

"I guess," he said, when the five of them were sitting over a plate of tacos, "that this is it, then?"

No one had to ask him what he meant.

"Nothing will ever be quite the same again," said Jasmin, with a catch in her voice. "I mean, school without Sanjay . . ." She threw him a loving glance.

". . . and Chloë – it'll be awful."

"I'll miss you," Sinead said, squeezing Chloë's hand. "You will write?"

Chloë nodded, not daring to speak.

"I wish," said Sanjay suddenly, "that we could press some huge Pause button right now, and be like this for ever. All five of us – you know, real mates."

"We can," said Jasmin.

They all looked at her as if she had finally flipped.

"That bit won't change," she said. "We will all still be friends wherever we go and whatever we do. What we have is special. It doesn't just stop because someone changes school or moves house."

"I guess," said Chloë doubtfully.

"I know what!" cried Sinead. "What's today's date?"

"The third of July," said Sanjay.

"Right!" cried Sinead. "Every year on the third of July, no matter where we are or what we are doing, we'll meet at Fat Harry's, OK? All of us."

"Cool," agreed Jasmin. "Even when we are all at uni?"

"Even," added Sanjay, throwing her a shy glance, "when we are all married?"

"We'll bring our kids . . ." added Sinead.

". . . and then when they are teenagers, we will all sit in a circle and moan about the company they keep," giggled Jasmin.

"And in a zillion years' time, when we are staggering around on zimmer frames with creaking knees and a total lack of dress sense . . ." began Chloë.

"Yeah," interrupted Sinead, "why is it old people suddenly lose the ability to co-ordinate their clothes?"

". . . even then," continued Chloë, "we'll meet every year. Make a pledge!"

She thrust out her hand. The others clamped theirs on top.

"What's the pledge?" asked Sanjay.

"Friends for ever, whatever, wherever?" suggested Chloë.

"Friends for ever, whatever, wherever!" they cried in unison.

And then they all swallowed very hard indeed and had another drink.

Sunday 8.00 p.m.
Walking home, I said, "I don't think he's that keen on her. What sort of kiss do you think it was? Was there actual lip contact? Or was it lip to cheek, or lip to corner of mouth?"

"I think it was lip to corner of mouth, but maybe it was lip to cheek?"

"It wasn't **full-frontal snogging** though, was it?"

"No."

"I think she went for full-frontal and he converted it into lip to corner of mouth . . ."

Saturday 6.58 p.m.
Lindsay was wearing a thong! I don't understand **thongs** – what is the point of them? They just go up your bum, as far as I can tell!

Wednesday 10.30 p.m.
Mrs Next Door complained that **Angus** has been frightening their poodle again. He stalks it. I explained, "Well, he's a Scottish wildcat, that's what they do. They stalk their prey. I have tried to train him but he ate his lead."

*"This is very funny – very, very funny. I wish I had read this when I was a teenager, it really is **very funny**."* Alan Davies

When Mr, 'hey, call me Dave'
Sissons suggests that 5B keep
a diary for a whole year,
reactions are decidedly mixed!
Yo! Diary! grants us exclusive
access to all areas of six very
different fifteen-year-old
minds:

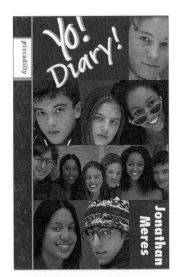

Seb – the rebel and
'Spokesdood for a
generation';
Meera – a girl obsessed
with astrology;
Steven Stevens – so good
his parents named him twice;
Clare – the local neighbourhood Eco Warrior;
Mandy – Ms Personality and Karaoke Queen, and
Craig – convinced that he's the only virgin on the entire
planet.

Jonathan Meres has written a riveting and hilarious tale of
teenagers teetering on the edge of the millennium! It's a
story of changes, drama, love, intrigue and plenty of good
old angst! And that's just in the first week!

*"Meres' strong, irreverent characterisation and sharp humour
(he was a stand-up comedian with his own radio show) make
this a book that will achieve an effortless follo..ing."*
Publishing News

If you would like more information about
books available from Piccadilly Press and how
to order them, please contact us at:

Piccadilly Press Ltd.
5 Castle Road
London
NW1 8PR

Tel: 0171 267 4492
Fax: 0171 267 4493

If you would like more information about books available from Piccadilly Press and how to order them, please contact us at:

Piccadilly Press Ltd.
5 Castle Road
London
NW1 8PR

Tel: 0171 267 4492
Fax: 0171 267 4493

about ballet. Any screeching in the sound system was quickly adjusted by the production crew. But so far, it didn't look like any other group had put the same time and effort into their numbers as the Beach Babes had. They were sure all their practice was going to pay off. Poppy thought that Caves 'n' Rocks were really good, despite what Lily's brother had said about their song, and so were an Abba tribute group – although they were not original.

Soon it was time for Lilac and the Mermaids to perform. Lilac got up on stage, followed by her band, and took the microphone. She looked very glamorous in a mini-dress and high heels. The rest of the

Mermaids were dressed much more simply so that Lilac looked even more stunning. Her long blonde hair had been newly styled and, with a flick of her golden tresses, she began to sing. Her song was: *Chocolate Sundae Girls*.

The Beach Babes couldn't believe what they were hearing. Surely Lilac didn't think she could get away with pinching their song.

granddaughters. But what was odd was that Mr Farrington, rather than looking happy for his daughter, looked rather disconcerted and puzzled.

Chapter Seven

Lilac did not sing brilliantly at all, but the fact that the song was good enabled her to pass it off quite well. Her friend Fern Zitelli was on guitar, with Lulu Lamont on drums, and they did a passable cover version of *Chocolate Sundae Girls* even though it was nothing like the Beach Babes' version and they had no backing vocals or dance routine to speak of.

The judges seemed very impressed. As far as they knew it wasn't a cover version of